"Come ..... he said.

"Where are we?" she answered. Her mouth felt numb.

Jason pulled the mug from Lyda's hand and poured the remainder of the tea on the ground, tossing the mug into the undergrowth.

"What are you doing?" she asked. "Where are we?"

He yanked her from the car and she felt helpless and weak and very tired. She sagged against the car, squinting up into the darkness. A huge dark shape loomed over them.

"What . . . ," she began, but Jason had flicked on a flashlight in one hand and caught her arm in the other. He was pulling her toward the shape.

A tower, she thought. It was a tower. She had seen it that first day in the graveyard with Lilli.

They went through a heavy door of rough wood and began to climb stairs that spiraled up the wall of the tower. The stairs went up forever, winding stairs out of the Brothers Grimm, past one floor and then another and then another. Lyda stumbled and pulled and reeled in the uneven light.

The tea, she thought. He'd put something in her tea. . . .

**Check out these other creepy reads from
Simon Pulse:**

The Party Room trilogy
by Morgan Burke

Desert Blood 10pm/9c
by Ronald Cree

Killing Britney
by Sean Olin

SWANS IN THE MIST

D.E. ATHKINS

Simon Pulse
New York | London | Toronto | Sydney

SIMON PULSE

An imprint of Simon & Schuster Children's Publishing Division

1230 Avenue of the Americas, New York, NY 10020

Copyright © 2006 by Nola Thacker

All rights reserved, including the right of reproduction in whole or in part in any form.

SIMON PULSE and colophon are registered trademarks of Simon & Schuster, Inc.

Designed by Steve Kennedy

The text of this book was set in Century Old Style.

Manufactured in the United States of America

First Simon Pulse edition August 2006

10 9 8 7 6 5 4 3 2 1

Library of Congress Control Number 2006925832

ISBN-13: 978-1-4169-0047-4

ISBN-10: 1-4169-0047-0

Married, Duck, isn't it funny? I wish I could see your face when you read this. He's nobody you know . . . but not nobody. Handsome, really. Older. Rich, of course. Very, because I'm very expensive. It's my job. More later.

xoxo

Lilli

"Married," said Lyda, turning over a small, thick sheet of cream-colored stationery as if she might find a definition of the word on the other side. But the only other writing apart from her name and the address of her boarding school was the embossed address of an unfamiliar hotel centered at the top of the single page.

"Married," repeated Lyda, more loudly this time.

Her roommate, Maryjane, looked up from the fortress of books on the bed around her. "Who?"

"My sister," said Lyda.

"That's the invitation?" asked Maryjane.

"The announcement," said Lyda, and shook her head in disbelief.

"You weren't invited? Pity party. Weddings can be very revealing. In many ways, it's human society at its most ritualistically primitive." Maryjane was planning to study social anthropology at college next year—while writing murder mysteries on the side.

Lyda shook her head. "I just can't believe she didn't invite me. Or at least let me know before she did it. I mean, how hard is it just to dial it in. . . ."

"Very interesting, don't you think?" Maryjane said, nodding. "What is she avoiding by cutting you out of this key human mating ritual? And the method. Formal paper, snail mail. What—"

"Stop it," Lyda warned.

Maryjane sighed. "Okay, okay, avoid the issue. Brood about it in secret and before you know it, kabam . . ."

"Now is good," Lyda said. "Or I'll show you kabam, all right."

"Oh, okay." Maryjane looked smug. "Just remember that when you decide to get married, you'll get to engage in your own primitive rituals, and then you can forget to invite your sister back."

"No," said Lyda. "No, that's not it."

"Mmm-hmm," said Maryjane knowingly, and returned to her book on the adaptive behavior of the criminally insane.

Lyda started at the note for a while, reading it over and over until she'd memorized her sister's words. Then she folded the note and put it in the small box of other letters and cards her sister had sent her over the years since their parents had died in a car wreck. They'd left a trust fund just large enough to pay Lyda's way to the right schools and Lilli's way out into the world. Lyda had been eight then, and Lilli had just turned eighteen. Now Lyda was seventeen, and her sister had just turned twenty-seven. They weren't at all alike—almost as if, in fact, they hadn't even had the same parents. But Lilli had always been protective of Lyda, in her way, and Lyda had always looked up to Lilli.

Still thinking of her sister, Lyda turned to her computer to scroll through her homework assignment without really seeing what was on the screen. In the early years, Lyda had spent summers at various camps and holidays at the homes of friends. As she'd gotten a little older, each holiday had become a traveling party. Lyda had joined her sister in apartments and flats, town houses and villas—once, even a castle—in cities throughout the world. Her sister had shared these temporary homes with other beautiful, carefully groomed men and women who didn't eat enough but had been generous to an awkward child. Watching quietly from the edges of strange rooms filled with strangers, Lyda had not been unhappy. And she learned lessons she'd never have gotten in school. Those had been Lilli's modeling years, years of reasonable success—although

Lilli had been more interested in having fun than success.

And neither success nor fun had ever included the idea of marriage. Lyda had no memory of their parents' marriage, but Lilli, who rarely spoke of their mother and never of their father, always said, "Marriage is for men, not for women." Whatever that meant. At any rate, the men Lilli loved—if it could be called love—had always been strictly flavor of the month, and Lyda had never met the same one twice.

In recent years, Lyda had seen less and less of her glamorous older sister—less in the pages of magazines, less in person. Lilli had never been into communications and plans. Arrivals and entrances were her specialty. Random phone calls, random e-mails, and now this.

Married.

Whom would someone like Lilli marry? The letter didn't even tell Lyda that.

Married. Later. xoxo Lilli.

Lyda smiled, shook her head a final time. Typical Lilli. No use in calling her. She probably wasn't even on the same continent she'd been on when she wrote that letter. Lyda would get details soon enough. Meanwhile, she had a European history test ready to grind her bones to make that troll history teacher's bread.

Lyda turned back to her computer screen. After a time, she managed to forget about her sister.

"You'll love her." The golden girl turned from the terrace that looked out over the famous harbor full of yachts and sailboats undoubtedly belonging to both the rich and the famous. She'd seen the view before, and from terraces just as imposing as this one. But never as a married woman. Never as a woman who wouldn't— *couldn't*—be gone the next day or the day after, had she felt like it.

She sipped the dark wine and tried not to wrinkle her nose. She liked champagne, but he said it was a drink for children. And maybe he was right. She wasn't getting any younger, and beauty didn't last forever.

But he loved her for more than that. He spoke of her courage, all alone in the world.

Her strength of character, which she supposed meant that she was one of the Eurogirls (she was *not* Eurotrash) who hadn't succumbed to drugs and alcohol and anorexia and all the other dangers and diseases that went with it. Spirit, he said.

He was marvelous. So handsome. So physically . . . good. She shivered as his fingers brushed hers, as he touched a finger to her chin and brought it up until her eyes met his.

Dark eyes. That vampire streak of silver hair. Older and wiser and he had chosen her and she had, finally, let him.

The eyes crinkled slightly—gray eyes the color of the antique dueling pistols mounted on the wall of the suite, she noticed irrelevantly.

"A sister?" he said, and she was surprised somehow that he hadn't already known, even though she'd been careful not to mention it. She wasn't sure why, but she'd felt uneasy about the idea. Somehow she'd felt that he wouldn't be pleased.

But that wasn't possible. Was it?

"My younger sister," she said. "Lyda." She

decided not to mention how much younger.

"Lyda," he said. "Lyda. Tell me all about Lyda."

He smiled then. And kissed her. He did it very well. He did so many things very well. She leaned against him, let him be in charge the way he liked it.

And was almost able to forget that feeling of something not quite right, something about Lyda. . . .

· 2 ·

I didn't do it. Whatever it is, I didn't do it.

Lyda barely kept herself from blurting this out as she sat down across from the Dean of Students.

Dean Bethany looked down at the papers on her desk, then back up at Lyda. She folded her hands.

Lyda sat up as straight as she could. She'd never been in the dean's office. She was quiet, well-behaved, and made good grades—a boring perfect student and careful to keep it that way.

So why did she have the sudden urge to

confess, even when she had nothing to tell, even when she was innocent?

Wasn't she?

"I'm sure you know why I've called you in, Lyda."

"Ah, well . . . ," Lyda said. The dean would tell her. She was, after all, the boss.

The dean tapped her finger on the stack of papers. "Since you are such an exemplary student, I don't have any problem with the request."

"Oh, good," Lyda said.

The dean smiled. "Jason Ducat," she said. "Your new brother-in-law."

Jason who? Thanks, Lilli, she thought. Lyda felt like an idiot. But she smiled back at Dean Bethany. "Of course," she said.

"His request that you have some time to visit and get acquainted, even though we are in midsemester, is unusual, but not impossible," the dean continued. "You've finished your midterms and you will be able to take assignments with you. And it is, after all, only for a week."

"A week," said Lyda.

The dean smiled her official smile again. "I understand a car will be here to pick you up tomorrow afternoon at three. Your tickets will be waiting at the airport. You've made visits with your sister before that have been arranged in this manner, so you're familiar with it." Tap, tap. The dean glanced down, up again. "But of course you have all the details. Have a safe trip. And please convey our best wishes to your sister."

The dean removed the top sheet and studied the one beneath it. The interview was over.

Lyda stood up. "Thank you," she said.

She left, but she didn't go back to class. She went back to her room, fell on the bed, and pulled the blanket over her head, refusing to remove it even when Maryjane returned, demanding to know why Lyda had been called out of class.

This time, Maryjane was more useful. "Jason Ducat," she said, "is your new brother-in-law?"

"According to the dean," Lyda said, her voice muffled through the blanket. "At least I *think* it's who my sister married."

Lilli's note had been tucked away in the box for almost two months, and no further communication had followed. No e-mails. No phone calls. Nothing. Every time Lyda tried to call her sister, she had gotten a NO SERVICE message.

But she got service now. Fingers already flying over her keyboard, Maryjane said, "Nice. Ah, here. Multinational millionaire. Hmmm. Hmmm. Yep, that's him. De-blanket and take a look." Maryjane spun the screen around.

Lowering her blanket, Lyda saw a familiar-looking model—not Lilli—glass in hand, head tilted, standing next to a man who had somehow managed to almost disappear into the photograph. The camera loved the model as she clearly loved it. *Had* loved it, Lyda remembered now. That model had disappeared into the dark side of the airbrushed, air-kissed world in which she'd lived. Thinner, thinner even than heroin chic thin when it was the fashion, and then . . . gone.

Unsettling, how people could disappear like

that. Lyda pushed the thought of the lost girl away and studied the screen.

The man, it appeared, did not love the camera. He was standing back, looking slightly to one side with a dark, brooding expression. Hard to see. Hard to read.

"Reclusive, elusive, wealthy. Not much information, at least nothing substantial. Just stuff that reporters make up on a slow day," commented Maryjane. "Ruthless. Takes over businesses, busts unions, raids retirement funds. Probably murders baby seals in his spare time. But he *is* nice looking. . . ." A few other photos flashed by, none of them particularly revealing. Somehow he was always in the shadows, half-turned away.

"Well, I'm going to meet him tomorrow," said Lyda.

Maryjane raised her eyebrows. "Interesting. Family togetherness? Post I-forgot-to-invite-you-to-my-wedding guilt?"

Lyda groaned and began to pull the blanket over her head again.

"If you're leaving tomorrow, going blanket

won't help," her roommate remarked.

"I like the blanket. The blanket likes me. We're happy together," Lyda said.

"Your sister gets the guy, and you get the blanket? Intriguing . . ."

Lyda sat up, threw off the blanket. "You are ill, you know that?"

"No. Just innately qualified for my career of choice."

"The criminally insane should be afraid."

"Thank you," said Maryjane.

Lyda gave up. She grabbed a piece of paper and began making a list. Books. Assignments— she'd pick those up tomorrow. Clothes. Where was she going, anyway? *Nice job, Lilli*, she thought.

"Have fun," said Maryjane. "Take notes."

"Right," said Lyda. "If I see any of the criminally insane, you'll be the first to know."

It wasn't a private plane. But she was flying first class. She drank champagne—not bad, but so not up to her sister's standards—and watched the late-afternoon shadows spread across an increasingly empty landscape. They were going west and north, and then she transferred to a prop plane at an airport she never heard of, no first class here—very little class in all, in fact—that let her out in a cold country with an airport that should have had a sign labeled NOWHERE above the main entrance.

But she wasn't in the middle of nowhere. Not yet.

A large man in a black coat crossed the salt-rimed asphalt as she walked into the fifties functional shoebox of a terminal. "Miss Marling." Without waiting for an answer, he took the overnight bag from her hand. "Any more luggage?"

She shook her head. Lilli had taught her long ago to travel light. "If it doesn't fit, it doesn't deserve the trip," Lilli said. And then she'd loaded Lyda up with new things for her return to school.

"I'm Stinch," the man said, leading the way out the front of the airport to a dark SUV that idled at the curb. He opened the door, caught her elbow, and guided her into the backseat.

"Thank you," she said, pulling her elbow free as politely as she could.

When he'd gotten into the front seat and started the car, she said, "Where are we going?"

Stinch glanced at her in the rearview mirror. "Northwind," he said.

A town. Or the name of an estate, which, if it was, had the charm of not being cute or pretentious: Dunroamin. Xtasea. Xanadu. She decided not to ask. Instead, she said, "Far?"

"Awhile," he said.

She didn't want to make him use up all the words he'd apparently been allotted for the day, so she leaned back and looked out the window. Night was falling fast. She wasn't sure, but she thought they were near the Canadian border. They passed the edge of a small community, lights from modest houses and modest businesses blurring by. Then they turned on to a narrower road that twisted up and down and up again. Another turn, and the road narrowed even more. Lights twinkled few and far between and farther and farther away. Then darkness reigned except for the headlights of the SUV pushing against it.

Lyda yawned and tried to remember exactly how long it had been since she'd seen Lilli. Over a year? Since the end of the previous summer. Lilli had been snow-bunnying that ski jump guy, some European Olympic hopeful. Nice, but like a lot of athletes, not long on conversation—in any language. Lyda had mentally given him odds until Christmas.

She'd been right, more or less. It wasn't Mr. Jump-off-the-Snow-Tower-of-Death Lilli had married.

Some of her sister's boyfriends had wanted her to call them uncle. She never had. *Uncle Jason,* she thought. I don't think so. Besides, he was her brother-in-law now. *Yo, bro,* she thought, smiling. From his photographs, she'd bet he wasn't the "yo, bro" kind.

She fell asleep and woke as the car slowed to turn up an unpaved but smoothly graded road. The road climbed a slight incline, then leveled out in a tunnel of trees that pressed close against the headlights on either side. A stop for a gate that swung open electronically and quickly closed behind them as they pulled away. Another short tunnel of trees, and then they were crossing what looked like a meadow dotted with the tall, dark firs. They climbed another slight rise, and there below was row upon row of windows lit from within.

"Northwind," said Stinch.

3

Lilli was waiting. As Stinch opened the door and climbed out, Lilli flew out of nowhere, crying, "Lyda! You're here! You're here!" Her sister hugged her so hard that Lyda gasped.

"Hi," Lyda managed to say.

"Were you surprised?" Lilli said. "I was. When Jason told me how he'd sprung you from school for a whole week! Isn't it fabulous? Aren't you glad?"

"I was more surprised you got married," said Lyda.

Lilli laughed. "Come see why," she said, and pulled Lyda by the hand up a broad, shallow flight of stone steps beneath a portico. A massive door stood open at the top, spilling light into the icy darkness.

"Jason," Lilli cried. "Jason, come meet Lyda."

A figure suddenly seemed to fill the door, blocking all the light. Stinch stopped and spoke, and the figure shook its head.

"Jason!" said Lilli.

Stinch shrugged and moved away. Then Jason Ducat looked up and smiled and moved aside to let them pass.

"So this is my new sister-in-law. You didn't tell me she was as pretty as you are, darling." He caught her free hand and pulled Lyda toward him. Lilli let her go.

Behind them, the door closed heavily.

Darling. Ick, thought Lyda. She held out her other hand to him before he could pull her into an embrace, and stood on her toes to kiss him lightly, once on each cheek.

She got the impression he didn't like it.

"I'm not anywhere near as pretty as Lilli," Lyda said lightly. "But, thank you. I'm so glad to meet you."

He looked down at her. His clasp on her hands tightened. "Well, you'll have to allow me to disagree."

She pulled her hands back, twisting a little to free them. She seldom thought of how she looked. She wasn't used to compliments.

Before he could speak again, Lilli said, "I'll take you to your room so you can get settled. And then it's time for dinner—you're starved, right?—and you can meet everyone else."

"Don't be late," Jason Ducat said.

Lilli didn't seem to hear. She tucked her hand in Lyda's elbow and guided her up the stairs.

"Everyone else?" inquired Lyda.

"Oh yes," said Lilli. "I've married you into a whole new family, Duck."

"Thanks for telling me."

"But I've been so busy! And we were traveling."

"And you couldn't call. Or write."

"But now I don't have to. You're here!" They reached the top of the first flight of stairs and turned down a hallway. It seemed to stretch on forever.

"This place is big enough to be a resort or something," Lyda said.

Lilli laughed. "Isn't it ridiculous? And the name. Northwind. But you know how people are about their family homes."

"In England and France, maybe," said Lyda. She was feeling tired and cranky and unsettled. That wasn't like her. She was a good traveler. It was one of the laws of being Lilli's sister. "Anyway, who is this new family I'm about to meet?"

Lilli laughed and shook her head in answer. "Here's your room," she said, stepping in and gesturing with a flourish.

"Nice," said Lyda. It was, too—a big, handsome room with a jewel-colored rug spread across the gleaming floors, a bed heaped with pillows and fluffy with blankets, two big windows framed by heavy curtains, a desk, a massive wardrobe with built-in drawers, and even a full length mirror in an ornate stand.

"And your own bathroom. With excellent plumbing." Lilli turned, raising her eyebrows and wrinkling her nose.

"Excellent," said Lyda, wrinkling her own nose. They were remembering a Christmas spent in Scotland, a place with wonderful sweaters and no central heating and what could charitably be called antique plumbing. The flavor of the month had been the second son of some kind of title—and a major twit.

"If there'd been more hot water," said Lilli reflectively, "it might have worked out, you know."

"No," said Lyda bluntly.

That made Lilli laugh again. She swooped over and grabbed Lyda, squeezing her hard. "I'm so glad you're here, Duck," she breathed in Lyda's ear, and then was gone, calling over her shoulder, "I'll come get you for dinner in forty-five, okay?"

"But," Lyda said, recovering her breath. She was talking to no one. She stepped out into the hall. Her sister had disappeared.

Lyda looked up and down the hall. Generic manor house. Practically BBC. But definitely centrally heated. So why did she feel a sudden chill?

She peered up and down the hall again. But no one was there.

She stepped back into her room and closed the door. She thought about locking it.

But that would have been impossible, because the door didn't have a lock. She stared at it for a moment, then sighed. *No problem,* she thought. Unless one of the family was criminally insane.

She smiled ruefully and went to test the hot water.

4

He appeared as they came down the stairs, stepping out onto the black and white stone squares of the entry hall silently, ruler of the chessboard. "There you are," he said, snap, his fingers caressing the surface of what looked like a gold pocket watch he held in his hand. He snapped it shut, restored it to his pocket.

Lilli's hand tightened for a moment on Lyda's arm. "And there you are," she said aloud. She ran ahead of Lyda to join him. He caught her chin and tipped back her head and kissed her. Then he let go and stepped away, keeping his eyes on Lyda as she reached the bottom of the stairs and crossed the hall to them. "Lovely," he said.

Lilli put her fingertips on the sleeve of Jason's jacket, caressing it as if to soothe him. He offered his other arm to Lyda and she took it. Beneath the soft fabric, his arm was like iron and she had the sense of him withdrawing from her. It was like holding a cat that didn't want to be touched.

She forgot the impression as he led them into a large room that at first glance appeared empty. Then Lyda saw three people grouped before a fire. A vivid young girl who looked about fourteen was poking the smoldering logs, her sharp, chin-length curve of brown hair half-hiding her face. In a wingback chair to one side sat a guy a few years older than Lyda. He was swirling a drink in one hand and flicking the pages of a book on the table beside him. Even in profile, Lyda could tell he was worth a look. Across from him in a matching chair was a woman in a sweater and a long, dark skirt. She sat very upright, her hands resting on the chair arms, her face turned toward the door.

She did not stand as they approached. "Victoire, Jon," she said in a low, commanding voice, her glance flicking toward the other two occupants of the room before returning to fix on Jason.

"There!" said Victoire, giving the fire one final jab and watching as it roared to life with sudden ferocity. Andirons seemed to come to life against the blaze, eyes flickering, and it took Lyda an unsettling moment to realize that they were shaped into gargoyles with glass eyes behind which the flames danced.

The girl turned then, a small figure dressed almost formally in a dark plaid velvet skirt and a white turtleneck, her tiny waist cinched impossibly tight with a soft twist of leather. Incongruously heavy cuff bracelets of gold weighted down her narrow wrists. Matching leather flats, and tiny diamonds twinkling in her earlobes completed the picture. She looked like a child in grown-up clothes.

The young man stood up reluctantly, setting

the book aside. He took a long drink from the amber liquid in his glass. He was wearing well-worn black pants and a heavy gray sweater that had also seen better days. His hair was dark and curling and looked as if he ran his hands through it a lot.

"Ah, at last," the woman spoke again, without moving. Her eyes flicked once more, this time to Lyda's hand on Jason Ducat's arm. Without quite knowing why, Lyda stepped away from him.

"My new sister," said the girl. Her voice was slightly high-pitched, but not unpleasant. She hurried forward and air-kissed Lyda on each cheek.

The man by the fireplace didn't speak.

"My daughter Victoire," Jason interposed. "And her companion Rebecca Lune. And last, but of course not least, my own son Jon."

The faint edge of mockery in Jason's introduction of him caused Jon's expression to change from bland observation to . . . hatred? No, Lyda was imagining that, because in the next instant Jon was smiling and was suddenly very good looking as he raised his glass in a silent toast to her.

"You must call me Rebecca," said the woman, but it sounded more like a command than friendliness. She did not get up even when Jason escorted Lilli to the other chair that Jon had vacated and settled Lilli in it.

"Victoire," said the girl. "Not Vicki or anything. Daddy abhors nicknames, don't you, Daddy?"

"Why choose a beautiful name for your daughter if you can't call her by it," said Jason. "Now, what would you like to drink, Lyda?"

Lilli said quickly, "Have some wine, Lyda. Jason has wonderful taste in wine."

"Seltzer, if you have it," said Lyda.

"Or champagne?" asked Jason. "Do you like champagne?"

"Yes," said Lyda. "We . . ." She stopped. *We*—she and Lilli—*love champagne. We both do,* she'd been about to say.

Victoire giggled. "Champagne is for children, Daddy says."

Jon said, into his drink, "Or for celebrations."

"Jon's right. Let's have some," Jason said.

"Wonderful," said Rebecca sounding as if she meant just the opposite. "I'll take care of it." She rose at last from her chair and left the room, taking some, but not all, of the chill with her. Silence fell.

"You don't really look much like Lilli," Victoire said suddenly. She was staring at Lyda, her lips slightly parted.

"No," agreed Lyda.

"I never had a sister. Just Jon."

"I never had a brother," said Lyda. She didn't add *just Lilli* because Lilli would never be *just* anything. And she was Lyda's whole family.

"Or a mother or father, either, did you?" persisted Victoire. "They're dead, aren't they?"

Victoire must already know these things, Lyda thought, and glanced at Lilli. Lilli shrugged almost imperceptibly, and Lyda knew she was on her own. "Yes. They were both killed in a car wreck when I was eight."

"My mother died when I was even younger," said Victoire, sounding somehow triumphant.

"I barely remember her. She was twenty-seven, just like Lilli. She fell down the stairs and landed right there in the front hall. It broke her neck, and she—"

"Lyda's not such a ghoul as you, Victoire. Spare her the details," Jon interrupted.

"I'm not a ghoul!" Victoire said, and Lyda half-expected her to stick out her tongue at her brother.

Lyda said, "I'm sorry about your mother."

Victoire shrugged. "It was her fault," she said, and turned away.

Lyda blinked, not sure she'd heard right.

She glanced involuntarily at Jon, but he'd returned to his meditation on the contents of his glass. At that moment, the door opened and Rebecca came in. Behind her, a slight, pale man carried a large tray holding a bottle of champagne swathed in a white towel, and glasses. He set the tray down and prepared to open the champagne.

"Champagne just for you, Lyda," Rebecca cooed.

"For all of us, Rebecca." Jason smiled. "To

toast our new family. You will join in toasting my new family, won't you, Rebecca?"

"Of course Becks will," said Victoire.

"Victoire, you're not to call me that," Rebecca said, accepting her glass of champagne from the servant. "You know your father doesn't like nicknames."

"Daddy doesn't mind as long as it isn't in the family." Victoire glanced up provocatively from beneath her lashes at her father.

"I prefer Rebecca," he said smoothly. He accepted the glass of champagne the servant handed him. The glass was different from the other flutes: taller, and with a wrought silver stem. He walked to Lilli's chair and she rose, taking the last glass of champagne from the tray. He toasted Lilli silently. They looked into each other's eyes.

Then Jason Ducat turned. "To our new family," he said.

And obediently, they all drank.

We who are about to die salute you, thought Lyda. Now where did that come from? Too much studying for her last history test on the Roman gladiators, she supposed.

They ate dinner soon after in what Rebecca informed Lyda in a proprietary manner was the informal dining room. Lyda would discover that this meant a room smaller than the formal dining room, with furniture not so dark or old, and a table not quite as big and shiny. It also meant that they sat in exactly the same order as in the formal dining room: Jason at the head of the table, Lilli on his right, Lyda between Lilli and Jon, and Rebecca and then Victoire on Jason's left, across the table from them.

The small man who had brought in the champagne served dinner to Jason while another man, younger and taller, waited on the rest of them. The dinner might have been in the informal dining room, but the service was formal, right down to the plates and flatware.

And Jason, Lyda noticed, had his own china and his own flatware, slightly different from everyone else's. *Phobic?* she wondered, half-remembering one of Maryjane's discourses on some philosopher who wouldn't talk with his mouth open for fear of germs. She filed it away under "Facts for Maryjane" as she responded automatically to a question from Jason. "School? Yes, I like it."

"She's a good student," said Lilli. "Not like me."

"I was away at school for a while." There was no mistaking the longing in Victoire's voice. "Until two years ago, when I turned thirteen."

Lyda did the math. Victoire was fifteen—sixteen, at the very most. But she seemed younger. "You're not in school now?"

"Rebecca takes care of that," Jason answered. "Excellently."

"I do my best," said Rebecca complacently.

"Homeschooled," said Lyda.

"I'm surprised you never considered it for Lyda." Rebecca addressed herself, schoolmistress-to-dim-parent-style, to Lilli. Before Lilli could answer, she added, "But I guess you need a more stable environment to give a child a proper education."

Lilli wasn't into meow mixing it up. She

said, "Lyda's school is pretty proper, believe me. She's got her eye on several very good colleges."

"And do you like sports?" Jason asked. "Skiing, perhaps? In this part of the world, we get a lot of snow. It's too late in the season now, but you'll like it next winter."

"Do you hunt?" Victoire asked.

"Don't interrupt your father, Victoire," Rebecca said firmly.

"Oh, I . . . ," Victoire began.

"Apologize," Rebecca said.

"I didn't . . . I . . ." Victoire looked rebellious.

"I'm sure Victoire didn't mean it," said Lilli.

Rebecca said, "She knows better than to . . ."

"No, it's quite all right, Rebecca. A little informality is to be expected when people are getting to know one another." Jason nodded at Lilli, his generosity a gift to his new bride.

Now Rebecca looked rebellious, Victoire triumphant.

Then Lyda's eyes met Jon's and she was shocked at the dark hatred she saw there— hatred so strong, she could almost feel it. She looked away and looked back, thinking she'd imagined it.

But she hadn't.

What did I do? she thought. *Why would he hate me so much?*

Or was it she who inspired that look of murder? It could have been any of them.

Then his face smoothed into blankness. He smiled a bland, meaningless smile. "Well, Lyda, do you? Do you like to hunt? To kill? My father does."

5

"So, married life. You like?" Lyda asked as Lilli escorted her back to her room at the end of the interminable evening. She had other questions, lots of other questions, starting with Jason, but she didn't want to ask them in the middle of the hall. Time enough for that chat when they got back to her room.

Lilli laughed. "Of course, darling. What's not to like?"

"I don't know. Living in the middle of nowhere in a house that you need a map to get around in?" *And living with a psycho stepson?* she added silently. *And a weirdo husband.*

"Not a map, darling. Just a compass!" Lilli laughed again, and Lyda couldn't help smiling.

"Right. A compass. I'll unpack mine right away," Lyda said. She glanced back down the hall. "So, who else lives at this end of the castle?"

"Rebecca and Victoire are on another floor," Lilli said, gesturing vaguely. "So's Jon, at the other end. Jason and I are just up the stairs, on the floor above."

"You mean I have this all to myself?" Lyda said, gesturing at the not quite miles of hallway. "Good to know if I decide to get naked."

"Central heating!" Lilli said. "Also good to know for getting naked." She stopped as Lyda pushed open the door to her room. The bed had been turned back, and a small fire danced in the fireplace.

"Nice, but they forgot those little chocolates on the pillow," Lyda said. She turned to see that Lilli hadn't followed her in. "Aren't you coming to tuck me in and tell me all the gossip?"

Long and ago and far away, Lilli had done just that—tucked a young girl in. Instead of fairy tales, she'd told her gossip—silly and glittering and exaggerated stories about people she knew, people Lyda sometimes met, too. In exchange, Lyda had told her sister the "real fairy tales" that she'd read in school and, as she got older, her own gossip about her own world. They'd sit up, talking and laughing, until very late—or until a disapproving flavor of the month called in a sleepy or cross or impatient voice and Lilli would make a face and roll her eyes and say, "In a minute!" and then they'd talk some more.

Tradition, really, Lyda thought. That's what you'd call it.

She looked at Lilli, beautiful and poised in the doorway. Lilli looked away, looked back, laughed. "Not tonight, Lyda." She wrinkled her perfect nose. "It's the married thing. It's late. . . ."

"Oh," said Lyda. Married. Is that what married meant?

"Tomorrow. And we've got a whole week!" Lilli blew Lyda a kiss and closed the door. Just like that.

Lyda stared at the closed door. "Lilli?" she

said. But Lilli was gone, flitting down the long hall and up the stairs to her husband.

Was this Lilli in love? If it was, Lyda wasn't sure she liked it. "What about me?" she said aloud. "What about my needs?" Then she shook her head ruefully. She *was* being a big baby. Her sister was in love and newly married. Of course that would change things. She'd just have to get used to it, even if she didn't like her sister's choice.

A few minutes later she was sitting in her pj's on the bed. The low fire made the room feel cozy. She punched Maryjane's number on her cell. NO SERVICE. She sighed. Maryjane would have loved the whole meet-and-greet scene, not to mention the dinner of the disturbed. In addition to Jon's possibly frightening hidden depths and Jason's undoubted phobias, Lyda had picked up on other currents with definite undertow potential. And she wouldn't mind some advice on how to keep from drowning.

Happy families are all alike, she said to herself. *And is that so bad?*

Of course she was tired. It was late. The

whole situation was high-stress. Probably in time, things would smooth out and they'd be a typical . . . what was the word? Oh, yes: a typical blended family. Jon would be the moody older brother. Victoire would be the spoiled younger sister. Jason would be the stern yet affectionate father figure. Rebecca would be . . . what would Rebecca be? The governess? Did people have governesses any more? Hmmm . . . well, anyway, they'd be a mostly typical blended family.

Typical. Not a word she'd thought of with Lilli. Lyda surveyed the room. Of course, if typical included all this, it wasn't bad.

What do I know? thought Lyda. *I've never been part of a family. Not a real family. I might like it.*

Tomorrow she'd take her cell phone for a walk, see if she could find a way to reach Maryjane. She yawned. It was so quiet. She wasn't sure she liked being all alone, having the whole floor to herself. On the other hand, she wouldn't have been thrilled to have Jon for a neighbor. Or Victoire or Rebecca, either, for that matter.

The thought made her glance at the door. No way she could ask about a lock politely, was there? Probably rude. Probably ridiculous.

She made a face, got under the covers, clicked off the lamp. The darkness fell like an avalanche. She pulled the covers up. She wasn't afraid of the dark.

But she stared into it a long, long time before she fell asleep.

She woke up, the covers half-off, Girl in Danger 101, knowing that someone had just touched her cheek.

Instinct kept her still. Instinct forced the breath in and out as if she were still asleep.

A bad dream. A hell of a bad dream, the light touch on the cheek. The light, cold touch.

A cat, she thought. Maybe there was a cat in the house.

She listened for cat sounds, for any sound. The silence, like the darkness, was absolute. Even the fire had gone out. It stretched on and on, the darkness and the quiet. She tried to see, but couldn't. Tried to hear, but heard nothing.

At last she allowed herself to move, to shift in bed as if she was turning over, waking up a little. She shifted again, then said to the silent darkness, "Hello?" And then, "Oh, wow. Bad dream."

She forced herself to sit up and fumble for the lamp switch.

Light pooled around the bed and she flinched, expecting . . . what? Jon with an ax? Victoire with a carving knife? Rebecca with a nice dose of poison, cooing, "Drink this"?

The room was empty. Of course it was empty.

She'd had a bad dream. Lyda checked the door, but it was closed.

"Bad dream," she repeated.

But the touch had been so real. And she wasn't a light sleeper. Dorm life had desensitized her to everything but fire and earthquake.

Usually, not even a bad dream could pull her back up to consciousness. But the idea that someone had come into her room in the dark to look down at her and touch her face was too disturbing to believe. Better to believe in bad dreams in strange houses after long, hard days.

Lyda lay back down and pulled the covers up. When she finally fell asleep again, it was with the light on.

6

"I trust you slept well, Lyda." Jason made it a
statement, not a question. "You were tired after
your trip."

"Yes," said Lyda. "I was tired."

She poured a cup of coffee and helped herself to a substantial breakfast from the large
display of food on the sideboard of the smaller
dining room. Lilli filled a thin china cup with
tea and wound her fingers around it as if for
warmth.

Since she'd come to escort Lyda to breakfast
that morning, tapping on the door and then
pushing it open without waiting for a response,

Lilli had been talking with breathless speed as if to make up for lost gossip time. Between her room and the breakfast room, Lyda learned that the breakfast room was for family, and when guests came to Northwind, breakfast was served in the formal dining room. She learned that Jason liked having company for breakfast, but wasn't very talkative in the morning. She learned that Northwind was enormous, darling, and bordered on an even more enormous wilderness that spread across the rest of the state to join another wilderness in Canada.

She learned, as she sat down at the table, that Jason once again had his own set of dishes and flatware, different from what was clearly the designated breakfast set.

Lilli had grown silent and uncharacteristically still. She stared into her tea like a fortune-teller, only lifting her gaze to stare into space now and then.

No one else was in the breakfast room. Sunlight poured through the windows, bright and somehow cold. Jason kept his attention on a newspaper open before him. Lyda discovered she was hungry. *Nothing like a bad night's sleep to build up an appetite,* she thought.

Jason looked over at her when she sat down with a second, post-breakfast cup of coffee. Before he could speak, Lyda smiled and said, "Which papers?"

He raised his eyebrows. "The *Journal* and the *Times*, at the moment," he said. He lowered the paper.

"No local press?" she inquired.

His smiled and he was suddenly, devastatingly, charming. She felt the force of his full attention. It was if she'd been cold without realizing it, and was now basking in warmth and light. "Never," he declared. "Gossip and car prices."

"But so much news starts as gossip," said Lyda. "And not everyone agrees on what news is important."

"I should think it would be obvious," he said. He smiled into her eyes. His smile said she was the only one the room. The only one in the world.

Good grief. He was her sister's husband.

Her brother-in-law. Old enough to be her father. But the vibe she was getting was neither brotherly nor fatherly.

She reeled herself back. Lilli was still meditating on a second cup of tea.

"Obvious to whom?" Lyda asked lightly. She leaned back in her chair as if the little bit of extra distance would make her charm-proof. "I mean, look at the motto of the *Times*: 'All the News That's Fit to Print.' It might as well be 'All the news that we decide is fit to print.'"

He smiled again and she looked away. His gaze was amused—and aware. He knew what she was thinking and found it funny.

She said, quickly, "And news in a small town is just as important to the people who live there, no matter how small the town. Even in a house this size, I bet you've got enough people, between family and staff, to make a little news."

"Gossip, certainly," Jason said. He'd pulled his watch from his pocket and opened it, his thumb running over the surface. "But maybe while you're here, you can start a newspaper.

The *Northwind Press*, say. Motto: 'We know which way the wind blows.'"

Wrinkling her nose, Lyda said, "Whoa. Lame."

"Lyda, don't be rude," said Lilli, emerging from apparent trance.

Lyda blinked, then tried to hide her surprise.

Jason said, "No, no, I'm enjoying getting to know my new sister. After all, I never had one. Especially a sister who is, I think, interested in journalism." His thumb caressed the watch.

"It's an idea," said Lyda. "After I own a vineyard in France and before I become the first full-on give-peace-a-chance president of the United States."

He laughed and stood. "Youth," he said to Lilli. "Isn't it wonderful."

The way he said it made Lyda feel ten years old and stupid. She felt her eyes narrow and she glanced up to see Jason watching her. He nodded pleasantly as he folded his watch away, then tapped the stack of newspapers with one meticulously manicured finger. "Help yourself.

When you're done, leave them here and they'll be taken to my library."

He went over, tipped up Lilli's chin, and kissed her. "You'll have to entertain yourselves today. Business all day, I'm afraid. I'll see you at dinner tonight, darling."

When he'd left the room, Lilli turned to stare at Lyda. "What's wrong?"

"I wasn't being rude," Lyda said.

"I know that. But Jason is more . . . well, European. Not accustomed to American manners."

Lyda stared at Lilli until Lilli, amazingly, looked down at her now-cold cup of tea. She shrugged. "Really, I'm just . . . I just want everybody to get along."

"Aren't we? I mean, I haven't sent anybody screaming from the room." Now Lyda felt uncertain. *Had* she been rude? Too bad, because it was the most comfortable she'd felt around Jason so far.

She said, suddenly, unthinkingly, "You didn't marry him for, like, security or anything. Money, or—"

"Lyda!" Lilli jumped up. "How can you say such a thing! Jason loves me."

And I love him. That was what the script called for. But Lilli repeated, "He loves me. I know he does. And . . . and Victoire and Jon just need time to get used to the idea."

Victoire and Jon. Maybe that was the problem. *And Rebecca.*

"How long ago did their mother die?"

"Mothers," Lilli corrected. "Jon and Victoire had different mothers."

"You're his third wife? How did I miss that detail? Oh, right, you didn't tell me about the wedding until afterward. Well, well. And the first two died, leaving him with an heir, but no spare, if it's sons he wants. I can't say I like those odds."

"Stop it!" Lilli's eyes flashed, and Lyda realized she'd gone too far.

"Sorry," she said quickly. "Sorry. Really."

As quickly as she'd lost her composure, Lilli regained it. "No worries," she said. "So, go get dressed—can you find your way back to your room?—and I'll give you the grand tour."

"I'll leave a trail of bread crumbs in case I get lost," Lyda promised solemnly, and went to put on warm clothes to wear out into the cold.

Sometime later, much later, beneath a pale sun slanting toward afternoon, they rounded a curve in the beaten earth path of an artificial wilderness. Odd sculptures of animals both real and imaginary peopled the wilderness, all too often anatomically correct. Gross, Lyda said. Magical realism, suggested Lilli. Doing a comparative size measure, Lyda had offered wishful thinking. They were laughing, but Lyda stopped in surprise.

A graveyard lay ahead, sandwiched between the artificial wilderness and the real one that stretched up the mountain behind the house. And kneeling in the graveyard, a beautiful tricolor collie wagging its tail by her side, was Victoire.

She looked up as they approached, her face empty of all expression.

"Victoire," said Lilli. "I didn't know you'd be here."

"No," said Victoire. She didn't move.

The collie darted toward them and Lyda bent to stroke the dog's soft fur, scratching underneath the leather collar with tiny gold studs and making the dog groan in pleasure. "What a beauty," Lyda said sincerely. "It's one of the problems with being in prep school—no pets. I always wanted a dog. Is she yours?"

"Yes. Mine." Victoire rose. Lyda had chosen jeans and layers for her outdoor tour of Northwind and been glad of it—until she saw Victoire. Lilli, of course, looked very town and country in her cashmere and tweed, but that was Lilli. Victoire, meanwhile, looked like a doll. She was dressed all in elegant black, a red scarf a gash across her throat, the strange gold cuffs on her wrists. It made Lyda feel big and clumsy.

As if reading Lyda's thoughts, Victoire's eyes flicked over Lyda and she smiled a small, demure smile of satisfaction. "Pan, heel!" She spoke sharply, and the dog instantly wheeled to trot back to Victoire's side.

"Beautiful and very well-trained," said Lyda.

"Yes," said Victoire. "My father doesn't like anyone who lacks discipline." She looked from Lyda to Lilli. "Dogs. People. Especially people."

"Good to know," Lilli said lightly.

"I'm surprised you didn't know already," Victoire said.

Before Lilli could reply, a voice nearby called, "Victoire? Victoire, where are you?"

"Your nanny's calling," Lyda said, paying Victoire back.

Victoire's eyes narrowed. But before she could retort, Rebecca strode up the gate of the small graveyard. "I've been looking everywhere for you," she said to Victoire, not even seeming to see Lilli or Lyda. "Come with me, please."

For a moment, Lyda thought Victoire would refuse. But the girl finally shrugged, snapped her fingers at Pan, and walked slowly away to join Rebecca, the dog trailing at her heels.

Only then did Rebecca nod in their general direction. "See you at dinner," she said, and then the two were gone.

Lyda walked over to the grave where

Victoire had knelt. A rosebush, bare in the cold air, twisted up from the plot. She bent forward to read the words on the granite marker.

"'Beloved wife,'" she read aloud. "'Loving mother.'" Below that were only the dates of birth and death.

Lyda turned to face Lilli, noticing as she did so that behind Lilli, far away across half-wild sweeps of meadow and field, was a sheet of water and, farther still, what looked like the ruins of an old tower. It looked grim, as if it had been left behind by the creators of all the darkest fairy tales.

"Who?" asked Lyda. "Whose beloved wife? Whose loving mother?"

"Victoire's," Lilli said, her eyes bleak.

Dark bird flew up from the water to circle the tower. *Not vultures,* Lyda thought. Geese? Swans? "Victoire's mother," she said aloud. "What was her name?"

"I don't know," Lilli said. "No one ever speaks about it. Sometimes . . . sometimes I wonder if Victoire even knows."

· 7 ·

"But . . . that's impossible!" Lyda said. "Jason must have told you."

Lilli shook her head and turned. "We should get back to house. My feet are freezing. How does hot chocolate sound to you?"

"I'm not a child," Lyda snapped. "Talk to me."

"There's nothing to talk about." Lilli had reached the gate. She pushed it, and it swung open easily. The graveyard, for all its desolate air, was well-tended. "I knew Jason had been married. But the one time I asked him about it, he . . . he doesn't like to talk about it. About losing them. It's a very sensitive subject."

"But don't you want to know what happened? I mean, two wives! Is the other one buried here too? Did she—"

"Drop it, Lyda, okay? Let's go back to the house." It was a tone Lyda had almost never heard from her sister.

"Fine," Lyda said. She added childishly, "What*ever.*"

She followed her sister out of the graveyard. They'd almost reached the house when Lilli tucked a hand under Lyda's arm. "Sorry, Duck," she said. "It is a little strange, I guess. But just give it time. When Jason is ready to talk about it, he will. And then I'll talk to you. Tell you all about it."

"Of course," said Lyda. But she didn't believe Lilli.

She didn't know what to believe, but for the first time in her life, she didn't believe her sister.

She was alone.

NO SERVICE. NO SERVICE. NO SERVICE.

"Can you hear me now," Lyda murmured in disgust. The phone answered NO SERVICE.

She went from window to window, first in her room, then in each room on her floor.

NO SERVICE.

She climbed the stairs to search for a signal, but she still had no luck. Each room—pristinely empty, immaculately kept—brought the same message. So intent was Lyda on making her useless cell phone work that she'd reached the end of the hall before she'd realized it. She looked up to see vases of fresh flowers blooming against the silk wallpaper on either side of the door into which the hall dead-ended.

She stopped. Voices murmured, and she thought, *Lilli's room. Their room,* and then some instinct made her push back into the nearest doorway. She opened the door, slid inside the room she'd just left, and eased the door swiftly shut as the voices became louder. The deeper voice was Jason's. The lower, husky voice was Rebecca's.

"Ridiculous," Lyda heard Rebecca say. Through the tiny crack between door and frame, she saw them now. They stood very close, Rebecca's face tilted up to his. He was smiling at her. Rebecca swayed slightly, as if she might lean against him.

"Ridiculous," he repeated softly, meditatively.

Then he brought one hand up and Rebecca smiled as she caught the palm of his hand and held it to her cheek.

"Whatever you need," Rebecca said, "I can give you. You know I can."

Lyda had almost cried out. But now, shock and something like disgust stopped her throat. She watched as Jason and Rebecca stood like lovers staring into each other's eyes.

Then Jason's other hand came up, and Lyda flinched. The hand clasped Rebecca's throat, and Jason raised his thumb to slide it along Rebecca's jawline, stroking it, stroking it as he'd stroked his watch.

Rebecca made a sound like a purr and leaned into the hand that held her throat. He slid his hand around to her hair and yanked her head back and jerked her against him. Then he was shoving her back, back toward the room where Lyda stood.

Without thinking, Lyda dove for the nearest
door and found herself in a huge, ancient
wardrobe. Her forehead cracked painfully
against the shelf before she realized she had to
stoop to fit in. She pulled the door almost
closed behind her just as the other door
opened.

He did not push Rebecca to the bed. He
shoved her face first against the wall on the far
side of the room, one hand moving up under
the prim skirt, the other still tangled in her
hair. Lyda heard Rebecca gasp, moan. She
heard Jason say in a low, cold voice, "Don't
move."

And then he was slamming her against the
wall with brutal and efficient rhythm while
Lyda crouched in her hiding place in the semi-
dark, her eyes closed now, her knees trembling, her breath as ragged as poor Rebecca's.

Poor Rebecca, she thought. *Poor Rebecca?*

It was over as quickly as it had begun, a
harsh final intake of breath, another choked-off
moan.

Lyda heard, incredibly, Rebecca's low laugh-

ter. She heard footsteps, *his* footsteps, leaving
the room. Only then did she dare to peer out
again.

Rebecca was leaning with her back against
the wall now. She had one hand raised to her
mouth, her index finger tracing her lower lip.
But except for her quickened breathing, she
showed no sign of what had just happened.

The door to the room opened again and
Lyda flinched, thinking Jason had returned.
But the figure that walked into her line of
vision was not Jason. It was Victoire.

The two stood watching each other. Lyda
couldn't see Victoire's face.

Rebecca's hand dropped to her side. She
said, "Victoire," and her voice was normal.

Victoire didn't answer.

Had she been standing in the hall, listening?
Had she heard her father and Rebecca? Seen
them?

"You should be resting," Rebecca said. "In
your room."

"I'm not tired," said Victoire. Her voice was
thin and excited.

"Yes, you are, even if you don't know it." Rebecca stepped forward and put her hand on Victoire's arm.

The girl wrenched free. "I'm not a child. I don't need you." Victoire turned, and Lyda heard rapid footsteps moving toward the bedroom door.

"That's not what your father thinks." Rebecca's voice cracked like a whip. The footsteps stopped.

"You know the rules," Rebecca continued. She crossed the room out of sight.

Lyda heard Victoire hiss, "Don't touch me. *Don't touch me.*"

"Daddy's little girl." Rebecca's voice was cool and mocking.

"Don't touch me! Don't . . ." Victoire's voice became a whine. Her footsteps seemed to falter, stumble. Then the door opened and shut, and they were gone.

The phone that Lyda forgot she was clutching rang in her hand and she leaped, frantically trying to answer it, silence it. What if they heard? What if they came back?

A voice threaded through a storm of static into her ear. "Ly-Lyda, it's . . . Ly . . ."

Maryjane's voice.

"Maryjane," Lyda whispered hoarsely.

But the call was gone. She punched the number in again and again, whispering, "Come on, come on, *come on.*" Maryjane would understand. She'd know what was going on. *What exactly did you witness?* she'd drawl. *Intercourse or outercourse? I mean, given your limited experience* . . .

Maryjane would help put things into perspective.

But Maryjane was far away. Unreachable.

Giving up, Lyda shoved the phone into her pocket. She closed her eyes and tried to think. She had to get back to her room. No, she had to warn Lilli. Warn Lilli—of what? Would Lilli believe her? Maybe Lilli already knew. Lilli had always been casual about fidelity. Maybe Lilli and Jason had an arrangement. Maybe she should wait for Lilli to tell her. . . . No, that was ridiculous, because if Lilli knew, why would she tell Lyda? How would that help—if Lilli wanted help.

Lyda's thoughts tumbled and collided. Her

head ached. At last she couldn't stand it anymore. She pushed the door open. It was late,
she saw. The light was fading. She'd go to her
room. Take a bath. A hot bath. Wash what she
had seen off her skin.

Then she'd . . . then she'd figure out what to
do next.

· 8 ·

"You aren't supposed to be taking a bath now," said Victoire, and Lyda almost fell out of the bathtub.

Victoire was standing in the half-open door of Lyda's bathroom.

"Haven't you ever heard of knocking?" Lyda demanded.

"I did. You didn't answer. What were you doing?"

"Enjoying some privacy," Lyda said pointedly.

The hint was wasted. Victoire remained in the doorway. She sniffed the steamy air. "And you're using bubble bath, aren't you?"

"Bath oil," corrected Lyda

"Daddy doesn't like it. His nose is very sensitive. So is mine."

"I'm sure he won't even notice."

"He will," said Victoire. She came into the bathroom, and Lyda stifled an impulse to try to hide somehow beneath the water. She grabbed a washcloth and made a pretense of washing.

"Boundaries," she said. "Another word. You know, like privacy?"

Leaning forward to examine the table next to the old-fashioned pedestal sink, Victoire said, "You have lots of makeup, don't you?"

"Not really."

"Can I try some . . . Oh, look at this!" She held up a tube. "What a pretty color."

Lyda took advantage of the distraction to stand up and grab a towel. She wound it around her and stepped out of the huge old tub.

Meanwhile, Victoire had applied a bright pink gash across her lips. She stood on tiptoe to examine the effect in the mirror above the washstand and Lyda was reminded of a child playing at grown-up games.

"How old are you?" she asked, careful to keep her voice light.

But Victoire was instantly defensive. "Almost sixteen," she said.

Lyda reached for the lotion and began to apply it. "I swapped some eye shadow for that lipstick with a friend at school," she said. "You ever do that with your makeup? When you were at school, I mean?"

Victoire rubbed the lipstick in carefully until her lips were pale pink. "No."

She pursed her lips, blew herself a kiss in the mirror, and then giggled.

More like a child than ever.

"That color looks good on you. Keep it," suggested Lyda.

"Oh! Can I? Really? You mean it?" The lip color disappeared with startling quickness into Victoire's pocket even as she spoke.

"Hey, it's just makeup," Lyda said, a little overwhelmed by Victoire's excitement.

"Yes. Thank you!" Victoire was smiling like a kid on Christmas morning as she followed Lyda into her bedroom.

The far, deep sound of a bell wiped the smile from Victoire's face. "I have to go. I have to get ready for dinner. I'm supposed to be resting."

She darted out of the room, leaving Lyda staring after her. *Resting,* she thought. Still? Had Victoire been ill? Was Rebecca a nurse as well as a teacher, then? Maybe that was why she'd left school. Maybe Victoire had been sick for a while. Perhaps that was why she seemed so young for her age.

Funny Lilli hadn't mentioned it.

But then, thought Lyda, remembering what she had witnessed earlier in the day, maybe her sister had other things on her mind.

Okay, she told herself. *Get a grip. It's not like you were born yesterday. So this family is a little . . . strange. All families are.* At least, according to Maryjane, they were.

Since she'd been raised more or less family-free, what did she know? She'd talk to Lilli later. Find out more about who was who in the house. See if she could figure out what to do by how Lilli reacted to questions about Rebecca.

And where was Lilli, anyway? Lyda hadn't seen her since they'd left the graveyard.

The graveyard. *Beloved wife. Devoted mother. Dead wife.*

Okay, it was like the twilight zone of families here. But she could handle it.

Lyda got ready for dinner. She'd just pulled on her shoes when Lilli knocked and came in. "Oh, good. I couldn't remember if I'd explained the whole Pavlovian bell thing Jason has going on here."

"I figured it out, more or less," Lyda said. She looked at her sister, looked away. Rebecca's cold hostility made more sense, now. She was jealous of Lilli. Had she wanted to be Jason's wife? But how could she compete with Lilli?

She saw them then in her mind, Jason and Rebecca against the wall, and thought, *That's how.*

Then she thought of her own sister with Jason and the thought sickened her as the thought of her sister and whatever guy she had chosen for entertainment never had.

Her sister was married to him. He could do whatever he liked to her and she couldn't leave.

No, no, that wasn't right. That was another century. Or this century in a country where women had no rights.

But Jason was treating Lilli well. Lyda would have known in an instant if it were otherwise. Her sister was radiant, in golden silk with tight-fitted sleeves beneath golden bangles. She wore gold-threaded slippers on her feet.

Lilly caught Lyda's glance at her shoes and giggled. "I know. Life without the crucial four inches—forget the seven—is hard. But Jason doesn't quite like me in my spikes. It makes me almost as tall as he is. Ego-damaging. So I try to limit my stiletto fetish to special occasions."

"They're nice slippers."

"No, they're not. They're boring." Lilli shrugged and pulled her white cashmere shawl up around her shoulders. "I'll have to live vicariously through your shoes...." She bent forward and pretended to reel back in shock. "Oh, my god, Lyda, what *have* you got on your feet."

"Shoes," said Lyda.

"Those are not shoes. Have I taught you nothing?"

"They're boots, then. And they're warm." Lyda was laughing now. This was the old Lilli, her Lilli.

"What has warm got to do with it? I have been a very bad sister not to keep you in shoes . . . There's the bell. We'll discuss this later. In detail. Come on."

"Just a minute." Lyda darted into the bathroom and snatched up a bottle of perfume and dabbed it lavishly behind her ears.

Take that, Jason, she thought, hurrying back to join her sister.

They linked arms automatically and matched steps down the hall, down the stairs, across another hall, and through a set of doors into the room where Lyda had met everyone the night before.

And there they were, almost unchanged: Rebecca in one chair, Victoire in another, Jon leaning against the mantel, staring into the fire. Jason was in the act of handing Rebecca a drink.

"Dinner and family and bears, oh my," Lilli

murmured mischievously before dropping Lyda's arm to make her entrance.

Jason handed the drink to Rebecca without looking at her. Rebecca stared up at him as he focused all his attention on Lilli.

She crossed the room to him and turned her face up to his. He kissed her lightly, his arm going around her. His eyes flickered as he glanced over his shoulder at Rebecca.

Rebecca did not conceal her anger well, Lyda noted. Her anger and, perversely, a small flicker of triumph. Then Rebecca caught Lyda's eye, and her own eyes dropped, the hungry, burning gleam extinguished.

Victoire noticed nothing. She studied her clasped hands in her lap. Jon saw something, Lyda thought, although what he saw, or knew, was anybody's guess. He drank deeply from the glass he held.

A little petri dish of emotions, all there, Lyda thought. Maryjane would have been delirious with happiness.

Liars and psychos and bears, oh my, Lyda thought, and followed her sister into the room.

• • •

Had he really not noticed until after dinner, not seen the faint sheen of lipstick Victoire had been wearing—which now, post-dinner, was mostly gone anyway—until they had returned to the great room by the fire?

Lyda didn't think so. She thought he'd waited, biding his time, until he'd gotten, what . . . bored? Or until everyone had felt too safe, too comfortable?

Lyda had been drowsing in a big chair near the fire, tired after a long day and too much thinking about things that she couldn't sort out; tired too, from the glass of heavy red wine Jason had insisted she drink with dinner. She hadn't liked the dark, almost bitter, taste of it, but she hadn't argued.

Now she felt oddly detached, and had decided that was good thing. She started trying to think of ways to escape the rest of the evening of family togetherness when, to her surprise, Jon had come to stand next to her chair. He didn't look at all like Jason, she decided. Maybe he took after his mother.

His dead mother. Who was buried . . . where?

Stop it. She half-yawned and slid her hand up to hide it.

"Hold that thought," Jon said so softly that she almost didn't hear the words. Her yawn turned into a little choke of laughter that she also stifled behind her hand.

Jon's mouth twitched at the corner, a stealth smile, and Lyda let her hand drop to smile up at him. No, he didn't resemble his father at all. Jon was much, *much* better looking.

Jason looked over at them, and then swung around. "Victoire?" he rapped out. "What have you done to your mouth?

Victoire's mouth opened, closed, then her own hand came up protectively. "W-what?"

"Is that lipstick?"

She nodded slowly, her eyes huge above her hand.

Rebecca stood. She walked over to Victoire and pulled her hand away.

"Makeup." Rebecca's voice was scolding, as if she were speaking to a badly housebroken puppy. "You know better. Shame on you."

Color flooded Victoire's parchment white skin, and then faded, leaving her paler than ever.

"It's mine," Lyda said. "I'm sorry if I shouldn't have lent it to her, but I didn't realize it would be a problem."

Victoire was nodding eagerly. "Yes, that's it. I was just trying it and, and I forgot to wash it off."

"How sweet of you, Lyda," said Rebecca. "But your sister is a model, and models . . . well, I do understand that models wear a great deal more makeup than Victoire will ever be allowed to wear. They can't help it." She said the word "models" as if it were interchangeable with "sluts."

Victoire looked around at all of them, a glint of desperation in her eyes. "She took a bath! Lyda did. In the middle of the afternoon. With bath oil!"

Lilli drawled, "Well, I guess you're going to hell, Lyda. Especially since you have a trashy model for a sister."

Rebecca set her own mouth in a hard, thin line. She glanced at Jason. "Jason," she said, her voice commanding.

"It's just lipstick, for god's sake," said Jon.

Pleasantly, Jason said, "I have my rules for a reason, Jon. Victoire, don't let it happen again."

Victoire scrubbed at her lips with her hand. "Isn't Lyda going to get in trouble? She broke rules too."

"What rules?" Lyda heard her voice and knew she sounded angry—but not nearly as angry as she felt. Rules from thin air, makeup phobias. Bath laws, for god's sake.

"We don't bathe in the afternoon," Rebecca said. "It puts a strain on the plumbing."

"Oh." That deflated some of Lyda's anger. She was vague about the plumbing, but it sounded reasonable. Or did it? Why would the plumbing not work well in the afternoon?

"And the bath oil? It smelled." Victoire made a face to indicate her innocent disgust.

"It was lavender, actually," Lyda said.

"I'm sure that Lyda didn't understand how sensitive I am to artificial scents. In the future, she'll naturally wish to respect my preference for a clean, wholesome appearance, especially in young ladies," Jason said. He tapped his nose and smiled almost playfully at her.

"Are you allergic?" Lyda asked.

Rebecca frowned. "That's not the issue," she began.

"Let us say, I am aware," Jason said. "And, unfortunately, unappreciative."

Lyda opened her mouth to say something, possibly to accuse Jason of being a nose fascist, and then thought better of it. She forced a smile. "Of course I'll respect your aversions." Aversions. Now that was a good word. Thank you, Maryjane. It sounded like perversions, and the more Lyda learned about Jason, the more she began to think that was his home address. "And if I do forget and smell like, say, L'Heure Bleue, I'll stay out of your way."

"Really," began Rebecca, her tone almost outraged. "You're . . ."

"Really," said Lyda sweetly. For Rebecca, Lyda didn't have to make a list and check it twice. Rebecca was naughty, not nice.

Victoire looked uncertain. For a moment, Lyda thought she saw Jon's mouth twitch before he raised his drink, but not in a smile this time.

Lilli looked amused.

Lyda met Jason's eyes. They were hard, gray flints. *He's angry,* she thought. Not used to even a little bit of "no" in his kingdom. The anger didn't bother her. He was on the list with Rebecca. She didn't like him. She didn't have to like him. She wasn't ever going to like him.

But she'd be gone in a week . . . no, six days, if anyone was counting. After that, she'd make a point of staying away from Jason. It wouldn't be hard. She'd be at school, he'd be here. She could spend holidays with friends. Then she'd be eighteen and answerable to no one. She had her trust fund to pay for college and she didn't need him.

She'd see Lilli without him.

Jason was watching her. They all were. She could feel it. But she didn't acknowledge it. A trick she'd learned from Lilli—never let your audience know you know they're captive.

She stood up, stretched, and smiled innocently at Lilli. "I'm wiped," she said. "So if you'll excuse me, I'm going to make an early night of it."

Boldly, she walked over to Jason and leaned up to kiss his cheek, still not quite seeming to see him. She sensed Rebecca's convulsive movement, felt the hard quiver of—revulsion? surprise?—run along her brother-in-law's arm as she momentarily rested her hand on it.

She leaned down and kissed Lilli's cheek on her way out. "Very bad Duck," Lilli murmured softly.

Smiling, Lyda straightened. "Good night, all," she said, and made her exit.

She thought she heard laughter as the door closed behind her.

Jason.

9

The crack of gunshot made her want to run.

"Pull," Jason said again, and another clay pigeon wheeled into the sky. He shot that one too. In fact, he'd killed every clay pigeon in sight.

Stinch took the empty gun from Jason and handed him a loaded one.

Farther down the range, Victoire was gunning at clay pigeons with intense determination. Her aim wasn't as good as her father's. He half-turned as she shouted in disgust at a miss.

"She gets too excited," he said.

Lyda stayed back. She didn't like guns. She

didn't like Jason with a gun. And she wasn't sure it was at all a good idea for Victoire to have a gun, in spite of Rebecca's close attendance.

Rebecca was shooting, too, taking turns with Victoire. Lyda noticed that she didn't leave Victoire alone with the loaded gun. Sharing the same gun meant when it wasn't Victoire's turn, she wasn't armed.

Jon, on the other side, was a good if unenthusiastic shot. He loaded his own rifle, taking his time and ignoring everyone else.

Lilli hadn't come at all. "You kids have fun," she'd said, waggling her fingers. "I'm going to enjoy being nice and warm reading by the fire."

"You'd rather read?" Victoire said in disbelief.

Jason had laughed. "Not all humans are hunters," he'd said. "Some are gatherers."

"Exactly," said Lilli.

Lyda had wanted to stay too. She had only one more day before she went back to school and she'd barely had a moment alone with her sister. But Jason had insisted, as he had insisted about so many things. She'd been horseback riding, an experience she did not care to repeat; taken many walks en famille; wasted an interminable evening learning to play bridge; spent two afternoons playing tennis on an indoor court. Jason had even held an informal wine tasting that had sent her reeling to bed early one evening only to wake up the next day with a thick head and a sandpaper mouth.

That had been the morning, she remembered a little bitterly, when he'd insisted on going riding.

Jason had, in short, taken a personal interest in Lyda.

"He doesn't need to school me, you know," Lyda said, in a rare moment of privacy with Lilli as she limped back to her room post-horse encounter. Lilli wasn't limping. She was an enthusiastic rider.

"Stick to it and you'll be riding in the hunt before you know it," Lilli had said unsympathetically.

"A fox hunt?" Lyda said in horror. "No way. And you wouldn't—would you?"

Not Lilli, not softhearted Lilli, who wouldn't even take modeling jobs wearing fur.

"No, I wouldn't," said Lilli. "But the hunt outfits are wonderful. I rode with one of the hunts in England once. I swear, the fox was a professional. Ran us ragged, then went to earth."

"Whatever that means," said Lyda in disgust.

"Means we didn't catch him. Or her, I suppose. . . ."

"No fox hunts. No hunts of any kind. And no more horses."

"Take a hot bath. You'll feel better."

"Is it allowed?" Lyda had asked.

Lilli had rolled her eyes. So Lyda had taken the bath. But not before she'd shoved a chair under her doorknob. She didn't know if it would work or not, but she'd seen it in old movies. And she hadn't been disturbed.

She found herself feeling sorry for Victoire. How crazy was it to be homeschooled—or whatever the megabucks class called it—in the middle of nowhere when you were fifteen years old? Little kids were more or less clueless about what to expect from life beyond the next toy, but someone Victoire's age must hate it—especially after she'd actually been out the world.

Not that Victoire had been completely nun-done at Northwind. She'd mentioned ski trips and expeditions to Paris and London, complaining of having to spend time in museums and how boring it had been to go shopping with Rebecca.

Jon, it appeared, came and went. He'd come into a small inheritance left by his mother when he'd turned eighteen a couple of years before—almost the same time that Victoire had come home.

She imparted this information as she dogged Lyda's footsteps, alternately friendly as a puppy dog or sullen—full of questions or full of warnings about what seemed to be an endless list of rules.

Lyda had discovered, however, that offering Victoire a lipstick or any other form of makeup caused her to vanish almost instantly. She'd grab it, exclaiming, shove it into a pocket, and disappear. Did she hide it in some secret stash?

Poor Victoire, Lyda thought again. The only thing the makeup ban was doing was teaching Victoire that makeup was everything, when it was only a game, a tool.

But it wasn't her problem. She'd be gone soon and with any luck, she'd seldom, if ever, darken this zip code again.

"Your turn," Jason said, and Lyda realized the shooting had stopped. They were all looking at her.

"Right," she said. She stepped up and gingerly accepted the gun.

Jason came up beside her. He leaned close to her.

He sniffed. "Ah, much better," he murmured. "Don't you agree."

What was the right answer? *Don't sniff me, you pervert?*

No.

He leaned in closer, put his arms around her, and raised the rifle to her shoulder. "There," he said. "You sight along here, you see? It's best to lead the pigeon a little, shoot just a little ahead of it. It . . . flies into the show and explodes. If you do it right."

She was trying not to breathe, not to feel him against her. She thought of Rebecca, pressed against the wall, of that awful rhythm, those awful sounds. She held herself rigid and yanked the trigger almost randomly when Jason called, "Pull!"

"You're not paying attention, Lyda. Shame on you. You can do better than that," he said. His voice was scolding, his grip painful as he forced her arms up.

"Pull," he ordered. His breath brushed her cheek, then he'd wrenched her bodily around, pointing the barrel not at the clay pigeon but at something flying low and fast near the edge of the field. Feathers flew up.

She reeled back, trying to break free, but he held her even more tightly. "Very good," he said.

"What was that?" she gasped.

"Just a pigeon," said Victoire, her voice seeming to come from far away.

"Your first kill," said Rebecca. Lyda turned

her head. Rebecca was staring at her. . . . At her
and Jason. Her face was pale. There was hatred
and an odd look of panic in her eyes.

Lyda turned away as best she could, trapped
in Jason's embrace. She saw then that she hadn't
killed the bird. It was on the ground, moving,
flopping brokenly. "It's not dead," said Lyda.

She looked down and saw that Jason's
thumb had started to move, stroking the sleeve
of her jacket inside the elbow, over and over
and over again.

He was excited, she realized. Bile rose in her
throat. If she puked on him, he'd let her go. . . .

"I'll take care of it." Jon spoke unexpectedly.

"No! Lyda needs to finish what she started."
Jason released her from his arms at last, but
not entirely. He began to pull her forward.

"No," panted Lyda. "No, I didn't mean to . . .
I didn't want to . . ."

She dug her heels in and jerked with all her
might and, for a moment, miraculously, she
was free. She turned to run, to get away.

"Don't be such a baby," said Victoire. "Just
kill it so we can finish shooting."

A hand caught her before she could escape. But it wasn't Jason's. It was Jon's. He hauled her forward so hard and fast, she almost fell.

"*We'll* take care of it," he said, walking rapidly away from his father.

"Jon!" Jon stopped, and Lyda almost staggered into him. She saw him turn, stepping forward slightly, somehow coming between her and Jason.

Was he protecting her?

"She has to finish the job," Jason said. "You know the rules. It wasn't a clean kill."

"And whose fault was that?" said Jon. He didn't wait for an answer, just turned and kept walking, dragging Lyda along behind him.

As they got closer to the bird, she closed her eyes, wanting to cry, wanting to apologize. How absurd she was—as if an apology mattered to the creature torn out of the air, still trying to make its wings work against the cold ground.

Jon said, "Hold on," and she felt her hands closing around the metal, the trigger.

"No," she said.

"It's the kindest thing you can do now," he

said. "Keep your eyes closed." He shifted her slightly and came up behind her as Jason had done, but although his hands were firm, they were surprisingly gentle. "Pull the trigger when I say to," he said in her ear. His voice was kind, almost soothing. "You don't have to look."

He shifted her again and she realized that, once more, he stood between her and the others . . . between her and Jason.

"Pull," he ordered, and she pulled the trigger.

The recoil pushed her back, and for a moment she thought she was going to fall. But he held her up. "Stay with me," he said. "It's not your fault. You did the right thing."

He held her until she was steady, and then turned her to face the others. She sensed rather than saw him bend and pick up the pigeon carcass. He made a sound of disgust, then flung it far into the woods.

She must have made a sound, because he said, "Something will make a meal of it. Its death won't be wasted."

"Will you hurry!" Victoire's voice came shrill and scolding across the stubble.

Jon led her back, slowly enough so that she could pull herself together. By the time she reached Jason, she no longer wanted to cry. She wanted to kill him.

But she kept her face runway blank. Jason said, "We'll make a sportswoman out of you yet, Lyda. You should have kept the pigeon, Jon. We could have blooded her with it."

Lyda had a vague idea of what he meant and just managed not to shudder.

"With a pigeon?" Jon's voice was cool, contemptuous.

Jason looked at him sharply, and then said, "Well, you're right. We'll save it for a fox. Or go hunting over the holidays where it counts."

She didn't answer.

"Nothing like it, a good kill," said Jason.

"Pull," Victoire shouted, and blasted another clay bird from heaven.

10

"It seems I owe you an apology," Jason said as soon as Lyda came in to join them before dinner that night. She'd arrived deliberately late. And she was drenched in L'Heure Bleue. The Blue Hour. It seemed a reasonable choice for the gathering. "Lilli has been explaining the error of my ways to me."

Lilli was standing next to Jason, her hand on his arm.

"It was a pigeon," said Victoire. "It's a sport."

"Not for Lyda. Not for me," said Lilli.

Lyda waited for Rebecca to weigh in with her opinion and her criticism, but Rebecca was silent.

"So I understand," said Jason. "I get carried away in my enthusiasms, Lyda. You will forgive me."

He wasn't asking her, he was telling her.

"How could I not?" Lyda said, and saw his eyes darken at her refusal to say *yes, yes, yes* and be grateful for the chance.

She remembered him pressed against her and she thought, *Pervert. Freak.*

She wished she could talk to Lilli about it, but she couldn't. The few words she'd managed to blurt out before making a dash for her room to vomit up what she'd eaten at lunch hadn't conveyed a fraction of the disgust she felt. Or the misery.

Because Jason was her brother-in-law. He was married to her sister, her only family.

She couldn't do anything about it now. She had to get away. She would get Lilli to come visit her at school. She would talk to her then.

"Well, then," he said. "Apology accepted." And then, shockingly, he laughed.

Lilli withdrew her hand from its resting place in the crook of Jason's arm and walked over to link arms with Lyda. "We'll have champagne tonight," she said. "It's your last night, and you've earned it. Don't you think so, Jason?"

Like Jason, Lilli wasn't asking a question, she was giving an order.

To Lyda's surprise, Jason obeyed. "Rebecca," he said, and Rebecca, who still hadn't spoken, rose from her chair and left the room.

Lilli led Lyda to a love seat and sank down on it, pulling her sister with her. She made it clear there was no room for anyone else. "We haven't had a minute since you got here," said Lilli. "Tell me what your plans are for the rest of the year."

With a shock, Lyda realized that Lilli was protecting her. She was grateful. But it was wrong, wrong that her sister was married to a man—to a family—who required that of Lilli.

She forced herself into chatter, laughter, silliness even. If Lilli could protect her, Lyda could return the favor.

After all, she was leaving the next day.

Lilli was . . .

Lilli was trapped.

• • •

Trapped. The word stayed with her. Later, much later, after an endless time trying to sleep after the endless evening, she got up to huddle over what was left of the fire. She was packed and ready to go, organized for a quick and efficient departure that would leave no trace of her presence. Nothing was going to stop her.

She gave herself a mental shake. Why would anyone try to stop her? She shouldn't make this into something it wasn't. Her sister had married a creep, a jerk, and all his money wouldn't change that. But Lilli had her reasons. Possibly she knew a side of Jason that no one else did.

"Not my problem," she said aloud, and pulled her robe tighter.

The knock at the door was so soft, she thought at first she'd imagined it.

It came again, and she sprang across the room to put her hand over the knob to push against whoever might be trying to push their way in. "Who is it?" she said.

"Me . . . Rebecca."

"Rebecca?"

"Open the door. Please, open the door."

"It's not locked. You know it's not locked," Lyda said, but she pulled the door back and stepped forward to block Rebecca's way.

Rebecca was still dressed in the clothes she'd worn that evening. Her hair had pulled lose from its severe knot and was half down around her shoulders. Her eyes were huge. "I've got to talk to you. Please. I need to talk to you, to tell you . . . you must let me in."

"Talk to me? You hate me," Lyda said bluntly.

"No! No. At least, I did. When she came, your sister, I hated her. We'd all been so happy here together. I thought we had. But then. You never know someone, do you? At least not until it's too late. Let me in, please."

The woman was nearly hysterical. Something had frightened her. Lyda stepped back.

"Thank you. I have to warn you, you need to know . . ." The words came in a rush, then stopped. Rebecca turned her head.

Her face went dead white, and Lyda thought she was going to faint.

"Did you hear that?" Rebecca hissed.

"Hear what?" Lyda asked.

"No," said Rebecca. "No . . ." She turned, looked back. "Be careful," she said. "Trust no one. No one, do you understand? No one."

She ran then, ran almost soundlessly down the dim, carpeted corridor. Lyda ran out into the hall after her just in time to see her disappear up the stairs at the far end.

For a long moment, she listened. But whatever Rebecca had heard was gone.

Lyda stepped back, closed the door. She pulled the chair in front of it and sat down in it.

"How weird was that?" she said aloud.

She thought about going to get Lilli. But getting Lilli would mean getting Jason.

She'd had enough of Jason, tonight and forever.

And possibly, Rebecca had too. Or maybe it was just a lovers' quarrel, although what she'd seen had had little to do with love. She'd been watching, listening to a power struggle against that wall, not love.

What had frightened Rebecca then? Had she

discovered her power was not enough? Had Jason told her it was over?

Good for Lilli, bad for Rebecca.

And it didn't make Lyda feel any more kindly toward him.

Lyda went back to bed and lay down, turning out the light. But sleep was even farther away now. Rebecca had been talking about more than a broken heart. She'd been afraid.

But of what?

Jason had used Rebecca, Lyda thought. Used her and, yes, abused her. If Rebecca had thought that was love, she was making the same mistake that many women made in the name of love. Women were stupid about love.

Lyda sighed. She hoped when she was stupid about love, she made a better choice than someone like Jason Ducat.

Poor Rebecca.

Poor Rebecca.

Lyda sighed again, and swung out of bed. She pulled on her robe and tightened the sash. She put on slippers.

She'd been to Rebecca's room once before,

looking for Victoire. She could find it again. She would try to talk to Rebecca and see if she could do anything to help.

But Rebecca wasn't there. Lyda knocked softly, then more loudly. No one answered. She glanced around. The hall was deserted. The whole house could have been empty, for all she knew.

Lyda turned to leave, then turned again. She turned the doorknob and the door opened. "Rebecca?" she whispered into the darkness.

No one answered.

Lyda cleared her throat. "Rebecca?" she said more loudly, and then, as loudly as she dared, "Rebecca!"

No one answered.

She looked in the direction of Victoire's room, one door down. Then she stepped into Rebecca's room and closed the door and, fumbling, flicked on the light.

The room was empty. Completely empty.

When she'd been here before, photographs had stood on the chest of drawers. Bedroom slippers had been tucked under the bed. Books had been arranged just so on the bedside table. They were all gone now.

Had she gotten the wrong room? No, this was it. Lyda recognized the curtains, the chair, the comforter.

She walked over to the fireplace and knelt down. The ashes in the grate were . . . damp. Someone had stirred the fire down to embers and then put water on it to put it out. It would be a mess to clean up.

Somehow, Lyda didn't think Rebecca would make that kind of mess.

"Rebecca," said Lyda.

But Rebecca was gone, as if she had never existed.

11

"Hi!"

Lyda sat up. "What?"

Victoire stood at the foot of her bed. "You have to get up," she said. "You're leaving today."

"I know," said Lyda.

"You can sleep on the plane."

"It's part of my plan." Lyda yawned and rubbed her face. "What are you doing here?"

"Rebecca's gone," Victoire announced triumphantly.

"How did you . . ." Lyda began, then stopped. "Gone," she said.

"She left last night. She was fired! Isn't that great?"

"For her, it might be," said Lyda without thinking.

Victoire stared at Lyda. "What a funny thing to say. She should have said good-bye, but I'm glad she's gone. She was bossy. A bossy bitch," Victoire added slyly, as if to see what Lyda would do.

Lyda ignored it. "How did you find out?"

"I went to her room this morning when she didn't come wake me up for breakfast and all her things were gone. So I went to my father's room—he didn't mind because it was sort of an emergency, you see—and he said they'd had a discussion last night and Rebecca decided to leave."

"I thought you said he fired her."

"Well, he did. He was just saying she decided to leave to be nice."

"How did she leave?" Lyda asked.

"How?"

"In the middle of the night . . . how did she leave?"

"Oh, she probably left early this morning, so no one would see her. Because she bossed everyone around, not just me, and they didn't like it either. So she was humiliated . . . humiliated." Victoire rolled the word around with satisfaction. "So she left before they could find out and laugh at her."

"I see," Lyda said slowly.

"Anyway, come have breakfast. We're all having breakfast together today before you go."

Victoire practically skipped out of the room.

It didn't make sense, Lyda thought, getting dressed and making sure she had everything packed. Or maybe it did. Maybe it did.

"But where did she go?" Lyda said. Two cups of coffee and she was Sherlock Holmes.

"Where? To her family, I assume. I was under the impression the two of you were not friends," Jason said. He raised the paper to signal an end to the conversation.

Lyda had already figured out that Lilli wasn't interested. "I hate to see you go, Duck," she said now.

"Duck," said Victoire.

"A nickname," said Lyda.

"Daddy hates—"

"Yes. Got it. But it's between me and Lilli, okay?" Lyda spoke sharply, and Victoire pouted. The newspaper twitched, but Jason didn't emerge.

"I like it," said Jon unexpectedly. "Only shouldn't it be a swan now?"

Caught off guard, Lyda laughed aloud. Lilli joined in. "She isn't a duckling anymore, is she?" Lilli said.

"Hey, I never was an ugly duckling," Lyda protested.

"No. The cutest," said Lilli.

"Well, I'm not going to be called Swan. You're stuck with the Duck, Lilli."

"Now and forever," said Lilli.

"You're all being silly," Victoire said.

The newspaper came down. "We should be going," said Jason.

"We?" said Lyda. "I thought Lilli . . ."

"You don't mind if I join you two, do you?"

"No," said Lyda. "Of course not."

"Good." He stood, kissed the top of Lilli's head, and said, "Then it's time to go."

He drove to the airport, the same block of a car in which she'd arrived. Daylight did nothing to add life to the scenery. Lilli told funny stories, carefully edited, about their adventures—two sisters and a stuffed duck around the world. Jason laughed and charmed and said all the right things, and as she turned from saying good-bye to him at the airport to face her sister, Lyda wished he was a thousand miles away.

"Bye, Lilli," she said, and hugged her sister hard. How thin she was!

Thinner even than her modeling days. Why hadn't she noticed it before?

"Bye, Duck," Lilli said in her ear.

And then Duck said, "Be careful," and turned to go back to her life.

"Where were you, the twilight zone?" Maryjane glanced up. As far as Lyda could tell, she hadn't moved from behind her stack of books since Lyda had left.

"Good guess," Lyda said.

"Did you study for the math test tomorrow?" Maryjane said.

"Yes. Even in the twilight zone, there is math."

"Good to know," said Maryjane.

"Are you studying now?" Lyda said. She unpacked as she talked, putting off the math as long as possible. But the math test was comforting, in a way. It was real, solid, logical. Not crazy.

"Nope. Finished." Maryjane held up the book she been reading. "Have you ever heard of Kraft Ebling?"

"No, and I don't want to." She squirreled away the last of her socks and fell back on the bed. "Math," she said. "Ugh. What is it good for?"

"Absolutely nothing," said Maryjane. "Especially if you are very, very rich. Did your new brother-in-law smother you in gifts?"

"Surprisingly, no."

"Affection?"

"Scarily, yes."

"This might be as good as Kraft Ebling," Maryjane said, sitting up. "Tell me."

When Lyda was finished, Maryjane said, "You know, you might think about getting a new family."

"Or no family. No family might be good— except Lilli."

"What it sounds like you've got here is a nice narcissistic personality disorder, if not a full-blown psychosis," Maryjane pronounced.

"You think?" Lyda said. She shrugged. "No, it can't be that bad. He's just a little, you know, spoiled. Entitled. Twisted entitled."

"Rich," said Maryjane. "As in, the more money you make, the more you get to make your own rules."

"You think . . . You don't think anything happened to Rebecca, do you?" Lyda finally spoke aloud the question that she'd turned over in her mind since the night before.

"She ran," said Maryjane. "Maybe he fired her, threw her out. Maybe they had a fight. Maybe he scared her. But she ran."

"You're probably right." Lyda picked up her math book. "So what do I do now?"

"Do?" Maryjane shrugged. "Nothing. Wait and see what happens."

"Wait," said Lyda. "Until the worst happens?"

"Which will probably be when your sister decides to divorce her husband of bad choice. She'll need all the support she can get."

"Right. You're right." Lyda flipped open her math book and tried to put Northwind behind her.

Spring had arrived when Lyda handed the package slip across the counter and examined the small box she got in return. It was from her sister.

Snagging a coffee at the caf, she headed for a corner and settled in. Lilli had become a regular e-mail wizard since Lyda had gotten back, sending news from Northwind two or three times a week.

Dull, dull news, with lots of exclamation points and words like "fabulous" and "wonderful," followed by more exclamation points. Not a writer, her sister. Never had been. But she promised to visit. Soon, underlined. xoxo . . .

A whole semester of it, just about. Lyda, in turn, had been careful not to mention her plans for spending the summer with Maryjane's family at their lodge in Maine.

Lyda tore off the last of the tape and opened the small box. A small, ridiculous stuffed swan fell out. It was all curved neck, floppy feet, enormous bill, and beady eyes. Lilli had scrawled on a folded piece of paper inside:

The Duck of the future is inside this swan. Hope she'll help you through the bad days (few) and the good ones (many).

xoxo

Lyda laughed, pleased. "Hey, Swan," she said. It was soft and plush, and she settled it carefully into her bag so it wouldn't get squashed.

Lilli, she thought, and shook her head. Lilli who had been a swan all her life.

• • •

Two days later, Jason stood up as Lyda walked into Dean Bethany's office.

"Sit down, Lyda," the dean commanded.

"What's wrong?" Lyda asked, ignoring the dean for the first time in her life.

"There's been an accident," Jason said. "We were doing a little rock climbing in Italy and . . . she fell. I'm so sorry, Lyda."

"How bad is she hurt? Where is she?" Lyda asked, not understanding.

"Sit down," the dean said, and guided Lyda into a chair.

Lyda sprang up immediately. "Where is she? I want to go to her. She'll need me. I'm her sister."

"Lyda," said Jason, his voice oddly flat.

"Dean Bethany," Lyda said, "I'll take my finals later, okay? Will that be okay?"

"We'll work it out," said the dean in a soothing, gentle voice.

It was the tone of voice that finally got through to Lyda. The dean never talked like this. Never.

"Dean Bethany?" she said, and heard how far away her voice sounded.

And how far away the Dean sounded when she answered, "Lyda, dear, I am so very sorry. Your sister is dead."

12

"No!" she screamed. And, "You're lying!"
And then, "It's a mistake, it's a mistake, I want
to see her." And then, "No, no, no." She'd been
given a sedative, with Jason saying in the background that he normally didn't approve of such
things and the dean agreeing as Lyda swallowed the pills the doctor had given her.

Then a drowsy, grief-sodden silent blur of
airports (where Lilli would never dash up to
her again shouting, "Duck! Duck!" and someone inevitably, involuntarily would duck his
head) and Stinch and the long drive through
the gathering darkness.

The door was opened by a housekeeper Lyda didn't recognize and Victoire and Jon stood before her, dressed somberly to match their somber faces. Lyda stared at them as they spoke. What could they say that would interest her now?

She allowed herself to be led to her room, which was unchanged, and lay down on the bed. She lay there through the dinner bell. She didn't speak when the housekeeper brought in a tray or when she came to take it away. She didn't move when Victoire came in, looking both lost and excited, and she heard only dimly random words that might be meant for comfort and that included the phrase "when my mother died."

She spoke only once, as Victoire was leaving. She said, "Lilli didn't deserve to die."

When Victoire turned a mute, questioning face to her, Lyda elaborated: "You said your mother deserved it, when she died. The first day I was here, that's what you said. I don't think anyone deserves to die. I know Lilli didn't."

Victoire said something else then, protesting? Explaining?

Lyda didn't listen. She didn't care.

Morning came and the drug had long worn off and the hell of pain filled her heart and soul. Lilli was dead, and she wanted everyone else to be dead too.

Jason came in when Lyda didn't go down to breakfast, and said, "You have to get up."

"No, I don't," she said. *Lilli's dead.*

"Get up, Lyda," he said.

"Or what? You'll use me for skeet practice? Push me off a rock, maybe?"

"You're upset. You don't know what you're saying."

"I'm upset and I do know what I'm saying." She folded her hands across her chest as if she too, were a corpse. "Where's Lilli? Did they do an autopsy? I want an autopsy."

"I had her cremated," he said.

Lyda gasped as fresh pain gouged her. "Burned," she whispered, and thought of medieval witches condemned to fire for being old and different and outcast—or young and beautiful and independent. "You burned her," she said. "You killed her and then you burned her."

"Stop it," he said harshly, and she might have been frightened except she was already dead. "Stop talking like this. Lilli was my wife and I loved her."

Lyda closed her eyes.

"If she's dead and you burned her, then why am I here?"

"We're having a memorial service tomorrow."

"Where?" Lyda asked, and found some small shred of comfort in the thought of seeing all of Lilli's friends, the ones who'd been part of Lilli's world and, some of the time, part of Lyda's, too.

"Here," said Jason, and the comfort ebbed away. She knew without asking that they would not be invited.

She ate some dinner that night because Jon brought it to her.

As he came in, Lyda said, "Okay, your whole family has been here. You can go away now."

"You should eat something," he said, and set the tray on the table next to bed.

Next to the covered dishes she saw the tiny bottle of champagne and said in a strangled voice, "What are we supposed to be celebrating?" and began to cry.

Jon said, "I thought Lilli would want you to have it," and she cried harder and harder and then she was wailing and doubled up and Jon was resting one hand on her shoulder, saying nothing.

Because, she knew, he knew there was nothing he could say at all.

After a long time, she stopped crying. She sat up and found that Jon was offering her a box of tissues. She blew her nose and rubbed her face dry and said, "Crying doesn't help. It doesn't change things."

"No," he said.

She looked at him and could see no trace of his father in him. She couldn't blame him for what she was sure his father had somehow caused, through recklessness or hubris or worse: the death of her sister.

But she couldn't entirely let him escape the consequences of being Jason's son, and like an angry, cruel child poking at a bruise, she said, "When your mother died, did it feel like this?"

He inhaled sharply and grew very still.

"Because Lilli was my sister, and when I was little she was like my mother, like this really cool mother and the other kids at school wished they had a mother like that, or even anybody in their family like that, and she was my whole family."

Jon shook his head, once. Then he looked directly at her so she couldn't look away. "My mother left when I was seven. She came into my room one night and kissed me good-bye and said she was going away and she'd be back to get me. I should be good, she said, and remember what she'd taught me about right and wrong, even if it wasn't what my father told me. But I should mind my father until she got back.

"I was a little kid and only half-awake when she came to say good-bye. I thought, some-how, she meant she was going out to a party.

She and my dad did that . . . went away for weekends to house parties or to New York or wherever. . . .

"When I woke up, she was gone and no matter how good I was, she never came back. I found out later she died in a clinic in Zurich. She was being treated for drug addiction, they said."

Lyda drew in her breath. She touched Jon's hand.

He looked down at her hand on his. "She was my whole family too," he said abruptly, and stood up. He looked down at her, his face inscrutable. "Eat something. Sleep. The memorial for Lilli is tomorrow morning. Jason is going to scatter her ashes in the graveyard."

"In the graveyard! No, that's not she would have wanted. She'd want to be at the ocean. Or . . . or near her favorite shops in Paris. Or . . . there was this place we went, in Italy. . . ." She stopped.

"It's what Jason wants," Jon said. And then, cruelly, "He likes to have his family around him."

She raised her white face to his and saw that

he was pale under his tan. What did Jon know? What did he suspect? Did he think his father was some kind of Bluebeard, as Maryjane had said?

He turned away. "At eleven. The service is at eleven. I'll come to take you there."

But it was Jason who came for her the next morning, Jason who knocked and waited until she went to the door, Jason who held out his arm to her.

He was dressed in an expensive dark suit and she decided, as she moved past him, ignoring his arm, that he looked more like an expensive undertaker than a man in mourning. She walked beside him without speaking or touching him.

When they reached the top of the stairs, she stopped in surprise. Faces turned up to them, the faces of strangers. Jason caught her hand and lifted it to the crook of his elbow and guided her down the stairs.

"My colleagues and friends," he said to her, and to the small assembly, "my daughter Lyda."

Someone moved suddenly at the edge of the group, and Lyda had a glimpse of Victoire's pointed face and widening eyes.

Lyda tried to jerk her hand free at his words. "I am not your daughter," she hissed.

He smiled at her, his smile sad and brave and full of lies. Just loud enough to be heard by those nearby, he said soothingly, "In my heart, you are. You're upset. Let me get you something." He led her to a table on one side of the hall and said to a servant, "Water," without releasing her hand. His hands were cold and unnaturally smooth.

"You're not my father," she said again.

"But I am. I have the paperwork to prove it. I'm your legal guardian."

She stared at him in shock. "No."

"Poor Lyda," he said. "You didn't think your sister would leave you alone and unprotected in the world, did you? I arranged to have the papers drawn up after we were married, as soon as I found out about you."

"No," said Lyda.

He smiled. He patted her hand, crushed in

the vise of his elbow. She took the glass of water and raised it to her lips, but her free hand was shaking so badly, she had to set it down.

Someone was approaching. Jason turned, turning her with him as if she were a puppet. He said softly, from the corner of his mouth, "You should be nice to your father, don't you think?"

13

They had gone—all the business associates and friends of the family. Not her friends, not her family, she reminded herself. She huddled over the cup of tea next to the fire in the great room and tried not to think that Jason was, legally, her family. Her guardian. He had power over her, over her money, until she was eighteen.

Once, eighteen had seemed not so very far away. Now it seemed an eternity.

Jason said, "You'll be leaving us tomorrow, Lyda."

She raised her eyes. "What?"

"Going back to school. Isn't that what you want?"

She nodded, instinctively afraid to show too much enthusiasm. She tempered the nod by saying, "At least to finish the school year."

"At least," said Jason.

"I wish I could go to school," Victoire said. She was taller than when Lyda had last seen her, less childlike. The malicious, childlike glee that had been one of her many expressions had vanished, leaving a permanent look of sly secretiveness.

She hovered over Jon now too, where before she'd seemed to ignore him. She was lonely, Lyda guessed. When Rebecca left, no one had replaced her, and Victoire didn't seem to be a girl who could entertain herself easily.

"Low motivation," Dean Bethany would have written on a school report. "Not a self-starter."

Almost the worst thing that could be said about a student at Dean Bethany's school.

Lyda frowned, and then pulled up an image. "Your dog, Victoire. Pan, that was her name, right? Where is she?" She could guess that Jason wouldn't allow a dog in the house, but at least Victoire would have some kind of companionship.

Victoire shook her head. "She's gone," she said.

"Gone?" Lyda asked. "Did she run away?"

"No. But she was bad. I let her in the house and she was bad and nasty and she shed, so she went away."

"I made more suitable arrangements for it," Jason said. "I think it was for the best. A disobedient dog is almost as bad as a disobedient child."

The words were chilling, and Lyda had a moment of sadness for the beautiful animal she'd met briefly. Then she found herself wondering what Jason had done with Pan. She shook her head.

School. It would be a relief to get back.

Victoire leaned over the arm of her brother's chair. "What are you reading?" she asked. Jon murmured something, and Victoire said, "It sounds so dull. Is it?"

"Not to me," he said, and turned a page.

She leaned forward and, with a quick motion, flipped the book out of his hands. It tumbled to the floor and he scowled as he bent to pick it up. "What did you do that for?"

"I'm tired!" Victoire said. "I'm tired of sitting around doing nothing. Let's do something."

Lyda stared at Victoire. Was she stupid, or just completely without feelings?

Jon said, "What we did today was go to a funeral, Victoire. That's enough."

His tone of voice as much as his words stopped her.

"Oh," she said. "Well."

"Why don't you go on to bed, Lyda," Jason said. "You're getting a very early start tomorrow morning."

"Yes," Lyda said, and stood up. "Good night," she said to no one in particular, but looking at Jon. "Good-bye."

Someone had touched her cheek. Someone was standing next to her bed in the dark. She woke with a gasp and remembered Lilli was dead and hoped for one wild second that maybe it was Lilli's ghost come back to say good-bye.

The light clicked on and Jason stood there. "Time to go."

"What time is it?" Lyda said, wide awake and wary now.

"Time to go," he repeated. "Get dressed." He stepped back.

She stared at him as he stood there. The touch on her cheek had been real and sickeningly familiar, and she knew that he had done it before, had stood in the dark by her bed the first night she'd come to Northwind and stroked her cheek with his thumb.

He stroked the face of his watch now, and she wanted to vomit. She swallowed the queasiness and said, "I can't get dressed with you here."

Snapping the watch shut, he ordered, "Hurry."

When he'd gone, she got dressed and folded the last of her things into her suitcase, placing Lilli's swan on top. She looked sadly at it for a minute, then squared her shoulders, picked up her suitcase, and went down the stairs.

Jason handed her a mug and she took it for the warmth. "Hot tea," he said, and she nodded.

Even though the beginning of summer was almost upon them, it was cold in the predawn chill. She shivered as she got into the car, careful not to brush against Jason, who stood holding the door open for her.

He slid in next to her on the driver's side. She cradled the cup and took tiny sips to avoid talking.

Jason didn't seem to notice. He drove slowly, past misshapen objects just beginning to step out from the background of the night.

The road dipped and narrowed, and the car bounced unevenly and slowed more. They wound in and out among the trees, and she felt her eyelids grow heavy. She was so sleepy. So tired. It was so early. She'd sleep on the plane, blissful sleep on the plane, where she could forget everything. Maybe she would sleep forever . . . like Lilli.

Lilli . . .

The car stopped, and Lyda raised her head with an effort as Jason got out of the car and walked to her side to open the door.

"Come here," he said.

"Where are we?" she answered. Her mouth felt numb. She had to hold on to the mug very tightly to keep from dropping it.

He pulled the mug from her hand and poured the remainder of the tea on the ground, tossing the mug into the undergrowth.

"What are you doing?" she asked. "Where are we?"

He yanked her from the car and she felt helpless and weak and very tired. She sagged against the car, squinting up into the darkness. A huge dark shape loomed over them.

"What . . . ," she began, but Jason had flicked on a flashlight in one hand and caught her arm in the other. He was pulling her toward the shape.

A tower, she thought. It was a tower. She had seen it that first day in the graveyard with Lilli. And yesterday at the memorial in the graveyard . . . without Lilli.

They went through a heavy door of rough wood and began to climb stairs that spiraled up the wall of the tower. The stairs went up forever, winding stairs out of the brothers Grimm, past one floor and then another and then another. Lyda stumbled and pulled and reeled in the uneven light. Her legs wouldn't do what she told them. It was like being stoned.

The tea, she thought. He'd put something in her tea. And fear numbed her further so that she did fall.

He hauled her up with a growl, and her shoulder felt as if it had been wrenched from its socket. Beneath the numbness of her legs she felt the pain where the stones had bitten into her shins and knees.

She tried to shout, to call for help, but he shook her viciously and marched her on, up and up and up the stone stairs of the stone tower, all the way to the top.

He pushed open another massive door and flung her forward and she fell, scraping her hands and bruising her knees. Then her face collided with stone and stars wheeled away behind her eyes and she spun with them into unconsciousness.

Lyda awoke in the gray dawn. She was thirsty and cold, and at first she couldn't remember where she was. She licked her lips and turned her head and winced at the pain in her shoulder and the soreness of her face. She remembered she'd gotten this wasted once before and had vowed never again to do anything so stupid.

She turned her head again, slowly and carefully, and realized she had kept that vow.

She wasn't in her dorm room. She was lying on a stone floor in a round room with the growing light of day pressing through the heavy barred glass of narrow windows.

"Jason?" she said. Her voice came out a croak.

She closed her eyes and let the world wheel away again.

When she woke the next time, full daylight filled the room, one bar of it across her face.

She pushed herself up. When the dizziness had passed, she looked around.

Piecing together memory with what she saw, she realized she was in the top room of the tower, a round room with three narrow windows of thick, leaded glass and heavy bars. A massive strap-and-beam door was the only way in and out. Along one side of the room was a mattress with a thin blanket on it. A heap of clothes was tumbled onto the mattress. She got up slowly and reeled as she fought to hold on to her balance. She half-knelt, half-fell onto the mattress and rolled so that she was half-propped against the stone wall.

She felt sick and cold and she hurt all over. She ran her thick, dry tongue over her lips and tasted crusted, salty blood. She closed her eyes again and drifted half-awake, half-dreaming.

She came to with a start, saying, "Lilli?" in a parched whisper.

No one answered. The room was bright above and dark below as if she floated on a raft in a well.

This isn't real, she thought, and closed her eyes again. But she opened them almost immediately. She was awake now, with no help for pain or memory.

She turned her head and lifted her hand. It didn't look like a real hand, blurred around the edges and so far away at the end of her arm. She squinted at it and wiggled her fingers.

"All there," she said stupidly. Lowering that hand, she lifted up something from the pile of clothes on the bed. Her clothes. She picked through them slowly, examining each item as if she'd never seen it before. All the clothes she'd packed for the trip to her sister's funeral were there, but that was it. No books. No makeup. Her shoulder pack with her cell phone was gone. Watch, jewelry, computer— all gone.

She'd been stripped of everything except her clothes.

And one thing more, overlooked perhaps, or considered unimportant.

Lyda looked down at it and, despite her terror, she smiled. She picked up the swan and cuddled it to her and whispered, "Hi, Lilli, I'm here. It's me. It's Duck."

She wanted to cry. But the tears had been parched from her body. She stared at the swan and fell into dreamless sleep as deep as a coma.

14

She came to with a start, half-slouched on the mattress against the wall. How long had she slept? Light still came through the windows, but at a different angle. And it was colder.

She got stiffly to her feet and made her way unsteadily to the nearest window. She could just see over the edge of the stone sill. She clutched it with sore fingers and stared. Her vision was better now, she noted dully. The sun was setting. From two windows she could see forests and far, far away, a field. From this window she could see Northwind, massive and menacing now against the mountain of firs that rose behind it.

She frowned. She was in the tower. Yes. Jason had brought her here at dawn. Was it the same day? Another day? How long had she been here?

Rapunzel, she thought, the word swimming into her brain. She reached out to grasp one of the bars across the window and pulled. It hurt her bruised, scraped hands, but it didn't move. She pulled harder, putting all her weight into it.

The pain shot through her, rousing her to something almost resembling normal consciousness.

Rapunzel, she thought again, and realized that, like Rapunzel, she'd been locked in a tower.

But I don't have the hair for it, she thought a little hysterically. Then she thought, *Jason locked me in the tower and no one knows I'm here except him.*

Why?

It was crazy. It made no sense.

She heard footsteps on the stairs and turned as the heavy bolt outside the door opened. "Jason," she said, but no sound came out.

Victoire pushed the door open and said, "Don't move. Stay right where you are."

Lyda stared. "Victoire? What are you doing here?"

The girl laughed, almost skipping in place. The wide-eyed, childlike expression was gone, replaced by a look of sly malice. "You were bad," she said, her voice almost a singsong. "Lyda was bad."

"Bad? I don't understand. Victoire, Jason—your father—brought me here. Locked me in. It must be some kind of . . . of mistake."

She didn't want to say "Your father's insane. Let me out."

"No," Victoire said, and set down the plastic bag she held. "Food and water," she said. She surveyed the round room curiously. "I used to play here when I was little. Fairy-tale games. Daddy would get so cross. He'd say he was going to lock me up in this old tower if I didn't behave myself."

"You need to let me out, Victoire. People will wonder where I am. They'll come looking."

But Victoire was shaking her head before Lyda even finished her sentence. "They won't. 'Cause you're with your family. Daddy's your guardian. That makes you my sister. Don't worry. Someday, you'll make a very good sister." Victoire spoke in rushed sentences, her face vivid with excitement, almost with glee.

Without thinking, Lyda took a step forward.

Victoire shrieked, "No!" and leaped back. The door slammed shut, and the bolt shot home.

"Victoire! Victoire, wait!" Lyda shouted, and flung herself against the door. It was like hitting one of the stone walls. She reeled back, moaning a little and panting as if she'd run a long way.

The room began to spin. Bending forward, she put her hands on her knees. "Victoire," she whispered.

Victoire was gone. Lyda was alone.

Slowly, she raised her head. Shadows were

gathering in the corners of the room. She shivered, straightened, and went back to the narrow mattress moored like a life raft along the far wall of the room. She pulled on her warmest clothes while she still had enough light to see, and then brought the bag of food and water to the bed. Peanut butter sandwiches. An apple. A soft plastic pouch full of water.

Had Victoire packed this school lunchroom food? Lyda examined it closely, not trusting it. But it was just peanut butter, just an apple.

She wasn't hungry, but she was very thirsty and thirst won over caution. She'd swallowed half the water before she realized she didn't know when—or if—food and water would be brought to her again.

It had to be, she reassured herself. He wouldn't leave her here to starve.

Although Victoire might. . . .

But why would he leave her here at all? Why? She propped herself against the wall, pulling the blanket around her shoulders. She tried to organize her thoughts, to think logically.

Logic failed her. Reason failed her. Reason and logic had no place in a stone tower in the wilderness. She thought of the miles and miles of dark forests around her and shivered. She pulled the blanket closer. The cold had crept in with the darkness. She was grateful that even in her numb despair at Lilli's death, she had automatically packed her warmest clothes for the trip to Northwind, remembering the grim chill of her first visit.

She wouldn't freeze.

She wouldn't starve, not yet.

She wouldn't die.

She examined that thought. *Lilli is dead,* she thought. She wondered if it hurt. Lilli falling, Lilli dying.

Lilli made into ashes by her husband. By Lyda's guardian.

Was dying so bad? It made more sense than this, than what had happened.

This was crazy, or she was crazy.

She lay down, making a cocoon of the blanket and her clothes. She tucked the stuffed swan against her chest with both hands. She rocked slightly from side to side, very slightly, so it wouldn't hurt and jolt her into feeling. The motion soothed her. She rocked and rocked, staring into the darkness as it grew and grew. The darkness frightened her. But then she got used to it. What difference did it make what hid in the dark?

She rocked herself to sleep, not caring if she ever woke up again.

The morning brought light and the bitterest cold before the dawn. In the iron gray chill before sunrise, Lyda woke shivering. She reached for covers that didn't exist and then remembered where she was. She unrolled herself from her cocoon, wincing in pain, and fumbled in her coat pocket to find a wool watch cap. She knew, although she couldn't see it, that the cap was knit in bright stripes. Maryjane had given it to her, assuring her solemnly that bright colors would make her easier to find in an avalanche.

Lyda pulled on the cap and tunneled back into her cocoon, pulling the hat down over her eyes and most of her nose for warmth. There, that was better.

She drifted into an uneasy doze, and then, as the sun brightened the windows, into a heavy sleep.

She awoke abruptly and pushed back the cap. She stared at nothing for a long time. Then she forced herself to sit up. She felt as if she'd come off a two-day soccer tournament, every muscle aching. She found the water and took a deep drink.

She gagged and for a moment wanted to vomit. But she willed herself not to.

For a long time, Lyda sat rolled in her cocoon, head bowed. She listened and heard faint sounds, birds waking up outside. Realizing that she was still holding the swan, she set it down on the bed next to her. Then, on second thought, she tucked it between the mattress and the wall where it couldn't be seen.

She got up and made her way around walls of the room, looking for . . . what? A secret passage? A handsaw and pickax? She came to a niche in the wall, wide enough for a person and deep enough to underscore how thick the stone walls of the tower were. Staring at the niche and then down at the rough hole tunneled into the rock floor, she realized at last what she was looking at: primitive plumbing.

Excellent plumbing. Lilli's words came back to her, and Lyda's eyes filled with tears. She wiped them away impatiently. She would not cry over taking a pee.

When she stood back up, she thought for a moment about that plumbing, about that movie she'd seen where the star had made his escape through the prison sewers. . . .

But this was a hole not much bigger than her arm.

Not yet, she thought, and moved on.

The ceiling of the tower soared away above her, all in stone. Finding a way to climb up to it wouldn't help, even if she had been a climber.

A climber. Rock climbing, he'd said. Lilli had fallen while rock climbing. But Lilli wouldn't have been caught dead climbing rocks. She'd had a bit of disdain for all the people who'd "gone Everest."

"It's about the gear and the bragging rights," she'd said, "trust me. If it doesn't have a lift, count me out."

Had Jason somehow changed her mind? People in love were stupid. But she wasn't even sure Lilli had been in love.

And Lilli had never been stupid.

She didn't know how long she'd been standing there, her hand resting on stone, when she heard him on the stairs.

She knew it was him. Something like panic raced through her, but she braced her hand flat on the wall and stared at the door unblinkingly as Jason unbolted it and came into the room. He was dressed as if for a business meeting, in a suit and tie. He had a notebook under one arm. He was immaculate as always. He repelled her and terrified her, and she hated him as she had never hated anyone in her life.

She didn't speak. She wasn't sure she could.

"Well, Lyda," he said as pleasantly as if they were at the dinner table. "How are you doing?"

Fighting down a hysterical urge to laugh, to try to reach him and gouge out his eyes, to scream and scream and scream, Lyda said, "I don't know. Apparently I've been bad." Her voice was steadier than she expected.

"Ah. Victoire," he said, and then was silent.

She waited as she knew he was waiting. Finally he shook his head. "I'm sorry," he said. "So sorry you brought this all on yourself."

"Excuse me?" Lyda said, not quite believing her ears.

"Lyda, Lyda, Lyda," he said. "I've always liked you."

She could think of several answers to that, none of them likely to get her released from the tower. So she kept quiet.

Jason sighed. "Well, let's get down to business, shall we?" The way his eyes ran over her made her straighten instinctively, ready to fight. He made no move toward her, however. "You are . . . lovely, even if you do not make the best of your assets. You are obviously a bright young woman. But you have so much to learn about what makes a woman a real woman."

Lyda felt suddenly ill. She said, "And you're going to teach me."

"It's my duty," Jason said simply, as if it was obvious. Again he waited. Again she outwaited him.

With a quick sweep of his arm that made her tense for fight or flight, he indicated the round room. "Consider this your school, your new school. Here you will learn what is really important: obedience, courtesy, respect, humility, neatness. Above all you will learn to be a dutiful daughter, to never give me cause to worry, or to be jealous the way"—he caught himself up, paused, and then concluded. "The way some people have."

"I'm not your daughter," Lyda said. She was so calm. Inside, she was screaming in panic, in rage, but she sounded so calm.

"You will learn to be," he said. And then, chillingly, "A devoted daughter. A beloved sister."

Or it goes on my tombstone? She almost said it aloud. But she didn't. Instead, she blurted out, "This is a joke, right? Lilli's death has made you . . . not yourself."

He shook his head. "Lyda. Oh, Lyda. You

have so much to learn." He held up the note-book. "This is a tool that will help you. It's your Book of Obedience. Say it."

She stared at him.

"Say it," he ordered.

"Your book of obedience," she repeated, lay-ing the slightest of stresses on the word "your."

His lips tightened. He reached into a pocket and Lyda thought for a moment he was going to produce a whip, or a gun. But he held up a pencil, a nub of a pencil. "In *your* Book of Obedience, you will write up all your failures and repentance for them. This is a primary exercise in your rehabilitation: acknowledging your failures and confessing to them. As you progress, we will add other exercises. If you fail, you will be punished."

"You're crazy! Insane!" It burst from her. She couldn't stop herself.

It was as if she hadn't spoken. He looked around the room. "Next time," he said, as if to himself, "I must remember to bring a chair."

He laid the book and pencil down on the floor. Then he said, "Turn around."

"What?"

"Turn around. Face the wall."

Lyda had a sudden image of Rebecca shoved against the wall of the empty bedroom. A shudder of revulsion broke through her. Slowly, reluctantly, she turned away.

"See," he said. "Obedience isn't that hard."

Then he was gone.

15

She slumped against the wall, staring at the notebook on floor. She didn't want to touch it.

He was insane. She knew that now. He was insane.

After a long while, she picked up the apple and ate it without tasting it. She drank most of the rest of the water. If she didn't, they might not think she needed it and she would need everything, everything.

She had to get away. She had to escape.

A rectangle of sunlight lay on the stone floor and she took her coat and spread it in the tiny patch of relative warmth. As the day passed, she followed the patch across the room, only getting up from time to time to look out each window in turn.

But she saw only forests and mountains and that far field from two of the windows. And from the third, Northwind. Once, she saw a tiny figure moving across the expanse of lawn. She shouted, knowing it was in vain. She hammered at the thick glass, then stopped. If she broke it, cold air would come in at night. If she broke it, Jason would know and . . .

You will be punished.

She stopped shouting. Beneath the window, just visible, a grass slope inclined to a small pond. She looked up again. The tiny figure had gone. Nothing in the landscape moved.

At dusk, Victoire came. Hearing her footsteps, Lyda hastily finished the last of the water and hurried to press herself against the wall behind the door.

"Lyda?" Victoire called through the door.

Lyda stayed silent.

"Lyda, answer me," Victoire said.

Moving around to face the door, Lyda said, "I'm right here."

"Go across the room. Stand by your bed."

Lyda moved back two steps.

"No!" Victoire shouted. "I can see you. Back up!"

Lyda frowned. How could Victoire see her? Was there a peephole in the door she hadn't discovered?

"Back up or I'm leaving and you'll starve."

Lyda backed up.

Victoire came into the room. She stopped when she saw the notebook in the middle of the floor. "Your Book of Obedience," she said matter-of-factly.

"Oh—you have one too."

"I used to. I still keep one, actually, just for myself."

Victoire's calm acceptance of the situation was worse, Lyda thought, than drooling madness.

"Throw the empty water bag to me," Victoire said.

Lyda obeyed. In return, Victoire set down a new bag of food.

"I'm going to need more than peanut butter and an apple," Lyda said conversationally. "And napkins would be nice."

"I know," said Victoire. "But you had to be careful not to eat too much yesterday. It might have made you sick."

"From the drugs your father gave me," Lyda asked bluntly. "What was it, roofies? The date rape drug of choice?"

Victoire's face flushed. "Don't say that."

"Don't say what? Date? Rape? Drug?"

"Stop it!" Victoire shouted. "Or I'll tell him. And then you'll be sorry. You'll be punished!"

The last word was a shriek. Victoire flung the food at Lyda, grabbed the empty water pouch, and ran out of the room, slamming the heavy door behind her.

She was little, but she was strong.

And also crazy, thought Lyda.

She went to the window to try to catch a glimpse of Victoire as she left. It was a long way back to the house. Did she walk? Ride a bicycle? Drive? Did Stinch drive her? Did Stinch know what was going on?

Probably. Bluebeard's sidekick, that was Stinch.

Lyda went back to her bed and ate dinner. Two sandwiches, this time. An apple and an orange. Something that looked like vegetable soup in a paper cup. A chocolate bar. Lunch box food again, but at least there was more of it.

She saved the orange and the chocolate for morning and went to sleep to have bad dreams that were still better than being awake.

You'll be punished.

I have to escape.

She lay in the sun again, feeling it against her face. Letting it dance against her eyelids. The notebook still rested on the floor, but she had picked up the pencil. On a pale stone, near the lower right hand side of the door where even a peephole could not see, she had made two marks, one for each night in the prison.

Nobody ever gets out of here alive. Who had said that?

But she would. She would.

She tried not to think of others, trapped in this place, who had never left. Best not to.

Best to know, just know, that she would be the one who did, who escaped and made sure that psycho Jason never escaped from anywhere again.

Why did this have to happen to me? she thought, suddenly, despairingly. But she knew the words to that riff: *The world just wasn't fair, so either kill yourself or deal.*

With her eyes closed, concentrating hard, she could imagine that Lilli was stretched out like a cat next to her in the sun on a beach. Big hats. Tiny strips of bathing suits. The smell of ocean and suntan lotion. The sound of laughter and gulls.

For a little while she half-dozed in her alternate reality.

Then she forced her eyes open. She'd go to the beach every day, she told herself, a little at a time. It would be better not to use it up too

SWANS IN THE MIST

fast. She got up to make her rounds of the windows: forests, forests with a single far field, the pond, woods, and Northwind. The view hadn't changed. And it still hurt to move. Bruises were just reaching their full potential along her legs and arms.

Did Jon know she was here? No, he couldn't. Jon wasn't like his father. Or his sister. Or maybe he was just better at concealing the wing nuts that held his brain together.

Still, Jon hadn't seemed to like his father very much. He didn't act as if he'd ever spent quality time with the Book of Obedience. But maybe, because he was male, he didn't have to. Males ruled, females obeyed, was that it? Men rule, women drool?

Not me, she thought. *Not me.*

She moved her coat to follow the sun. She stared at the notebook. When the sun got just over halfway across the room, she'd eat her orange and her chocolate and have more water.

The Book of Obedience. She stretched her arm out slowly and drew it toward her. What would she write in it? What were her sins? To imagine that, she would have to see the world through Jason's eyes.

The thought made her want to gag. The thought of writing in that book, of cooperating, made her want to gag.

She pushed the book away again.

No.

"Burn in hell," she said aloud, and turned her face to the sun.

16

He placed the chair by the door and folded his coat neatly over the back.

She sat on the mattress, her back against the wall, and folded her hands in her lap.

The book lay on the floor between them.

"Pick it up and bring it to me," he said.

"No," she said.

He stared at her.

She stared at him.

He sighed sorrowfully and shook his head. He got up, picked up the book, and opened it to the blank first page. He closed the book. He walked back to the chair and put on his coat.

He tucked the book under his arm, picked up the chair, and walked out of the room.

Victoire did not bring any dinner that night.

Hunger woke Lyda early. And cold, cold because, she suspected, she was hungry.

She lay in the sunlight that day and remembered a spa she and Lilli had gone to once, where all the fabulously thin and photographed were going to get fabulously thinner for more photographs.

Lilli hadn't chosen the "Cleansing Menu." They'd eaten well, although sparingly enough— tiny expensive plates filled with amazing tidbits. And in between they'd been massaged to jelly by supple, androgynous creatures clad in what appeared to be lab coats, sweated in saunas and lolled in mineral baths, had facials and manicures and pedicures.

And even lost a couple of pounds, oh so painlessly.

Welcome to the Tower Spa, thought Lyda, and followed the sun.

Jason came in the late afternoon. She sat down on the mattress when she heard him coming. She'd been right the day before—he didn't order her to face the wall if she was sitting down a safe distance from the door.

She was a little light-headed.

He put the chair where he'd put it before. He folded his coat over the back and sat down. He placed the notebook on his knees.

They stared at each other.

After a while, he said, "You poor, lost child," and stood up. He put on his coat, tucked the notebook under his arm, picked up the chair, and left.

Victoire didn't come that night either.

The next morning it was thirst, not hunger, that woke her. Thirst was going to be a problem. Her tongue felt too large for her mouth.

She lay in the sun and thought about water and felt cold, then hot.

The third day, they repeated the ritual. He only shook his head this time before he left.

Victoire still did not come.

Lyda lay awake all that night, cold and hungry. And thirsty. She tried to tell herself that this was nothing compared to what some people lived with all the time. But her body wouldn't listen to her brain. It screamed for water, making her dreams into nightmares that matched reality.

The morning brought rain, water she couldn't reach, water pouring down outside, water dimpling the lake, water falling from the sky. She listened to it fall in a kind of delirium, hearing the sound as she had never heard it before—not as background music to a cozy day spent drinking coffee, or talking with friends, or studying in the library, but as the most important sound on earth, a drumming that matched the pulsing in her veins.

Water, water, water, her body called. *Water, water, water,* the rain answered, soaking the world with what it needed most.

He was winning. She was losing. He could let her die. He *would* let her die.

But she couldn't let herself die. She wanted water. She wanted to walk in the rain. She wanted to walk out of her prison. She wanted to live.

She *had* to live. She had to get out of there alive.

To live, she had to obey the commands of a madman—or seem to obey.

Obedience meant food and water, that was clear.

She would obey. She would wait.

She would walk out of her prison and leave him here, somehow, to listen to the rain.

She would live. And somehow, he would die.

She would escape. One way or another, she would escape.

That day when he sat down, she kept her eyes lowered. To look at him would be to reveal the hatred that burned in her as fiercely as the thirst.

The hatred was warm. She wouldn't let him have that. Her voice when she spoke came out in a soft croak.

"May I . . . may I please have the Book of Obedience?"

Through her eyelashes she saw the look of triumph. "May I please have the Book of Obedience what?" he prompted.

She thought for a moment, confused, and

then realized what he wanted. "May I please have the Book of Obedience, sir?" she said.

"Very good, my dear daughter . . ."

She hated him. She would kill him. She kept her eyes down.

"Are you sorry you defied me?"

"Yes, sir," she said.

"You may have the book." He stood, walked to the center of the room, and placed it on the floor. "You may not realize it now, but you've made a very important first step. Confession is good for the soul. A pure soul in a pure body . . . there is nothing more beautiful, nothing more desired."

She said, "Yes sir," and was surprised she didn't choke on the bile she felt rising in her throat at the satisfaction in his voice.

He did not speak again, but his presence made her skin crawl. She clasped her hands tightly together until they shook with the effort, white knuckle against white knuckle.

She listened to the sounds of him leaving. She would not ask for water. She would not ask for water. She would not beg. . . .

He was gone. Would Victoire come now?

Lyda got up and took the notebook, setting it to one side of the mattress, careful not to let the notebook touch the mattress, as if it might contaminate where she slept.

Water, she thought. And the rain fell.

Victoire came that evening. She brought food. She stood in the doorway, swinging the bag of supplies. Lyda wanted to lunge at it, but she didn't.

Outside, she heard the rain slacken.

"I told you," said Victoire. "I told you that you'd be punished."

Lyda shivered, and it wasn't entirely acting. Victoire was part of her father's madness. Had she been born that way, or had he made her so? *Nature or nurture?* she wondered, remembering a science class from so long ago, so very far away.

She heard the bag hit the floor. Lyda hated Victoire, but not as she hated Jason. She raised her eyes slightly and said, "Thank you."

Victoire cocked her head. "You're very bad," she said. "Worse than your sister. The worst one of all. You deserve everything you get."

She spun and darted out, slamming the door behind her. Victoire was very good at slamming doors.

Lyda lifted her head then and stuck out her swollen tongue. Then, shaking and burning, she retrieved the supply bag and drank. And ate.

Then, to the gentle sound of rain, she slept.

The next day Lyda sat in the sun pretending she was in her weirdly enthusiastic math professor's class while he discoursed on the beauty of integers and negative numbers and she wrote random thoughts in her math notebook.

But it wasn't her math notebook that lay just outside the light. She would write her thoughts for nobody.

At last she picked up the book and the pencil nub. She opened it.

"BOOK OF OBEDIENCE," she wrote at the top of the first page. She started to write the date, but stopped. She didn't want him to know that she knew what date it was. So instead she wrote "1" in the upper right corner.

I've been a very bad girl, she told herself, trying to channel Victoire. No, Icky Vicky. That was her name now, Icky, Sicky Vicky. IckVick. Yes. She liked it.

IckVick has been a very bad girl and wants to please her daddy. Sicky Vicky who still wrote in such a book, who would do anything for her father's attention.

If Jason punished, he also rewarded, thought Lyda. How did a man like that reward a daughter like Victoire?

The image of Rebecca flashed into memory, and Lyda shook it off. Shuddered it off.

No.

Lyda wrote: "I disobeyed Jason. I wouldn't write in the Book of Obedience. I deserved to be punished." She stopped. She thought about writing that being punished had made her see things more clearly, but decided it was better not to encourage him.

What else could she write? Okay . . .

"I was rude to Jason in the past. I know I was upset when . . ."

She couldn't write "when Lilli died." She

thought, and then went on, ". . . when I came back to Northwind, but that is no excuse. Actions have consequences . . ." (one of her physics professor's favorite sayings) " . . . and I must bear the consequences of my actions. I very wrongly blamed Jason for the accident, but I know it wasn't his fault. It was a tragedy that he suffered too."

Not like he's going to suffer, she thought. *Sick bastard.*

"I hope he will forgive me."

She watched him read the book. He tapped the page with one long finger. "Good enough, as far as it goes," he pronounced at last. "But why do you call me Jason?"

"Sir?" she said.

He shook his head. "You resist the natural order of things. Well, well, I suppose it is understandable. Although I would think, alone in the world as you are, that you would be grateful I take a fatherly interest in your moral well-being."

"But . . ." She stopped herself. "I'm sorry, sir. I don't understand."

"No, you don't," he said. He sighed, the sigh of a long-suffering, disappointed man. "But at least you appear to be trying. Think. Ponder. I have given you the gift of time in which to do so, and space in which to do it." He paused. He repeated, "A gift."

"Thank you, sir," she said, realizing what he wanted.

"Very well," he said. "Keep trying."

To Lyda's relief, she got dinner that night and it was more substantial than any of the others: cold vegetable soup and bread with butter and more fruit and water. She was able to save the soup for the next day and part of the bread as well.

And she had a minor triumph of her own. Victoire was turning to leave when Lyda said, in her sweetest voice, "Victoire? That plastic bag by the door? I just put the paper and orange peels and everything in there. Garbage, you know? You don't mind taking it with you, do you?"

For a moment, Lyda thought Victoire might refuse, so she added, "Cleanliness is next to godliness, right? I'm sure your father would agree."

That clinched the deal.

And so IckVick became Lyda's garbage collector.

Lyda made sure to say thank you.

It took Lyda a long time to figure out what Jason had been saying. He spent several days reading her confessions, sighing his martyr's sigh.

"You're a smart girl," he said musingly after several days. "Can it be that you do not want to learn?"

"No sir," she said.

"And yet, my child, you do not. You do not take advantage of the gifts I have given you."

She felt a little rill of panic, a skitter of fear along her skin. She had to fight to keep her voice steady and calm.

"I only want to do what you want me to do, sir." She wanted to wash her mouth out with soap, but she said it.

"Do you?" he said. Sadly. "Do you, my child?"

He left her, then, to a long and hungry night.

She played his words over and over in her head and hated him for that, too. She did not like to think about him at all. She was learning to write quickly, to fill up the pages with variations on a theme: She was wrong, she was sorry.

He didn't like to point out her failings, but she was learning to pick up clues about what displeased him. He wanted to see her meager belongings all lined up in order, the same order every day. Her posture, her position on the mattress, the same every day.

She was always very sorry. Very grateful.

And most grateful of all that he stayed where he was, that his only caress was verbal: my dear. My child.

My child.

She straightened and reached for the pencil. She got it. At last she got it.

Lyda wrote: "I am sorry to have upset my father by not realizing that he would welcome me calling him that. I have not had a father in so long, I am not used to the idea. But it is a wonderful thing to have a caring father to look after you."

Yuck, she thought. *You are the father of hell, not my father.*

She cast her mind back over the whole time she had known Jason, made her see herself through his eyes. She practiced seeing the world through his eyes. Jason's world. It gave her gave her the creeps, but it also gave her a shred of power. He could not imagine her, could not even see her except through the eyes of his dark madness. *Insane people don't imagine,* she thought, *they believe what they see.*

She tried to imagine a world without imagination, caught herself, and smiled a little.

I am Jason, she thought. *I am looking at me and I don't approve of . . .*

And she wrote on.

Food and water came again, and Victoire sly and triumphant and suspicious and angry.

The days slid by with numbing sameness. Lyda studied Jason as a dog studies its master, aware of signals that the human has no idea are being sent. When she displeased him, Victoire would bring food without chocolate or fruit, or no food or water at all.

Once, when Lyda forgot and exclaimed, "But I never said that!" to Jason, Victoire brought water laced with salt. As she spit it out, Lyda thought she heard Victoire laughing, spying on her through the hidden peephole. Lyda almost hurled the pouch and its contents at the door, and then stopped. Instead, she used it to wash out clothes and, the next day, penitent and humble, dared to ask Jason for water for that purpose.

He surveyed her room—his kingdom—and said, "You have been learning the value of order."

The blanket was neatly and precisely tucked in around the mattress. Her clothes were folded just so, organized by type and then color on the floor.

He looked down at the floor. "And the floor could be cleaner. . . ."

"I could too, sir," Lyda said, pushing her luck.

"You become cleaner each day, my dear," he said, and to her horror, leaned forward and kissed her on the forehead. She almost jerked away. Almost.

She saved herself just in time, sat motionless as the dead beneath his lips.

She felt unclean, violated.

Did he sense it? Revel in it? Enjoy her submission and her revulsion?

Did he gloat over his prisoner, his prize? His *daughter*?

Nevertheless, the next day, Victoire came a little earlier. She brought a bag of rags, a cake of harsh soap, and three pouches of water.

"Thank you," Lyda said, and almost meant it. She handed Victoire the garbage and smiled. "I really appreciate it."

IckVick stared at Lyda. "Not like the soap you're used to, is it?" she taunted. "And where's the stinky perfume?"

"There are more important things in life than perfume," Lyda said, folding her hands and lowering her eyes. "Our father has taught me that."

"He's not your father!" she spat. "He's mine. MINE!"

And the door slammed again.

Lyda thought about Lilli as she cleaned. She brought out the swan for company and talked to the plush toy as she first washed her clothes, then the floor. Swan had become her Wilson the volleyball.

"What do you think?" she said to Swan, wringing out the clothes over the toilet hole. "A three-star establishment now? Oh, the meals aren't up to it yet? Okay, okay, two stars. But they manage very well, don't you think, considering the distance from the kitchen."

Summer had begun now, and at dawn the next morning Lyda saw for the first time that a pair of swans had settled on the small lake.

It's a good omen, she thought, and glanced over at her own Swan.

"Thank you, Lilli," she whispered, and went with almost a light heart to write more lies in the Book of Obedience.

· 17 ·

She sat at his knee, her face turned up to him.
The room was dark and full of shadows, lit only
by a fire, but she knelt upon rich carpet and the
walls were lined with glass-fronted shelves filled
with books and curious carvings and statues.

"Do you love her?" the girl asked. "Do you
love her more than me?"

"Of course not," he said. He stroked her
cheek, her forehead. She swayed beneath his
hand.

"But you spend so much time with her," the
girl murmured. Her upturned face was like a
flower in the gloom.

"Because I must. Because she needs me. You understand, don't you?"

The girl nodded because she was allowed no other answer. But her face, pretty enough, twisted for a moment into a feral mask of hatred.

"Jealousy, jealousy," he chided. "How will you ever be the beautiful young woman you were meant to be if you allow jealousy to rule you? You must learn to share in every way."

"I know," she said contritely. "I'm sorry."

He cupped her chin in his hands. "My child," he said. "My beautiful, almost perfect child."

And added, almost to himself, "You're growing up so fast. You won't be a child much longer."

She'd thought it would be hard to fill the Book of Obedience with confessions. Instead, it grew easier and easier. She wrote a girl she didn't know into the pages, a girl she would never be. Each page, each lie, made her stronger.

She became a fiction writer.

It was a way to fight the madness. Because

madness lurked all around her, and not just in
Jason and Victoire. It would take her too, if she
weren't careful.

She practiced telling time by the sun, prop-
ping the pencil up as a sort of sundial. She
traced the movements of the sun against the
sky and kept a record of where it was each day,
writing in tiny, secret letters on a scrap of clean-
ing rag. She watched the swans endlessly and
saw deer come and go from the edge of the
pond. She saw foxes too, and in the early
evening an occasional raccoon. Once a hawk
lashed from the sky into the meadow and bore
away a mouse or vole so quickly that she would
have missed it had she blinked.

The swans nested and cygnets appeared on
the lake one day—seven solemn, ridiculous
babies bobbing along in their parents' wake. It
was another sign, Lyda believed, a gift somehow from Lilli.

When she wasn't watching and listening,
inventing Lyda the Bad in the Book of
Obedience, Lyda made up elaborate dances,
pretending that she was preparing for a tour

with a modern dance group. In her version of modern dance, any movement was legitimate and Lyda leaped and spun and soccer side-stepped around her prison.

Tiring of that, she picked a tiny opening in the hem of her coat and hid her notes inside it, not realizing that it was a time-honored hiding place for all the poor and the hunted.

All that she did, she knew, was an act of defiance, and each act of defiance kept her strong and sane and fed her anger and disgust.

But Jason didn't know that. He "allowed" her to sit close to him while he read now, and she endured his nearness with downcast eyes. She engaged in little acts of wrongdoing in order to have confessions to make: a corner on the blanket not quite square, a spelling error.

She was careful not to make major mistakes, however. Almost as much as she hated him, she feared him. And she was fed little enough, growing thinner, ever thinner. A day without food and water would hurt her more now.

One day as he read, turning the pages with one hand and absently stroking the face of his

pocket watch with the other, Lyda blurted out
without thinking, "What time is it? Sir?"

He looked up, his face darkening with a fury
that took all her strength not to shrink from.
"That is very rude, to ask the time when you
are with me," he stated.

"I—I'm sorry. Sir," she stammered. She
reached out a hand, feigning timidity, as if
she wanted to touch him but was afraid to.
She knew she was safe. He didn't like to be
touched, for which she was deeply grateful. So
far, she didn't know how he felt if he was the
one who did the touching, for which she was
even more grateful. "It's just that you had your
watch out and I thought . . . maybe you were in
a hurry."

"You thought I was being rude?"

"No! I mean, no sir."

He frowned at her, and then said, "Well, it's
not a watch, so your accusation is unfounded."

"I wasn't accusing you. I swear I wasn't, sir."

"Swearing is unbecoming in honorable
young ladies. You are presumably telling the
truth and therefore don't need to swear."

She couldn't win. She said, "I'm sorry, sir."

He unexpectedly held out the watch. Although the chased gold case was the shape and size of a pocket watch, it opened to reveal something dark and thick curled within. Fur? Or a lock of hair? He drew back his hand too quickly for her to tell for certain.

She was afraid to ask, afraid to speak. She remained kneeling at his feet, mute.

"Beautiful, isn't it," he said. "From my first kill. My blooding." His eyelids dropped as he remembered. "I was luckier than you, my dear. It was a clean kill. It spared much suffering. Always remember that: Your mistakes cost others as well as yourself."

She bowed her head as if in agreement. She felt him watching her. She kept her head down, her hands folded and still. Was it animal fur his thumb stroked so compulsively? Or was it a curling lock of dark hair? The vile thought, the vile image, kept her mute.

At last he stood. She quivered like a rabbit trying not to run and excite the dogs that hunted too close by. If she stayed absolutely still, she might live another day. If she moved, if he touched her, she would run screaming to throw herself against the walls, to bloody her hands against the stones, to hurl her body at him and make him kill her as she wanted to kill him.

A trophy. He carried a trophy of his first kill with him always. What had he killed? How?

"You'll have much to think about, much to write about, my child. . . . I look forward to our lesson tomorrow," he said.

"Yes sir," she said. She did not look up until he was gone.

That night, something got one of the cygnets. There were only six when she looked out of her window the next morning. She leaned her head against the wall and mourned silently. She hoped the end had been quick. Had the hunter needed food? Perhaps it hunted for babies of its own. . . .

Poor baby, she thought, and wanted to cry for the little lost swan. For herself. But she would not allow herself the luxury.

Lyda was careful never to be near the window whenever the time for Jason or for

Victoire to visit drew near—not only because she didn't want them to know of her interest in the swans, but also because she had a new project to occupy her days, one that did not involve obedience.

Lyda was working away at one of the panes of glass in the window, using a chipped bit of rock to loosen it. But she had to be very, very careful. She didn't want to break the window and risk a day or more of starvation. They fed her regularly now, but just enough. Nor did she want them—him—to know that she contemplated anything that might seem like an escape.

Of course she couldn't escape through the square of leaded glass. But she could smell the scent of summer; hear clearly the sounds that came from the swans on the lake, maybe even figure out a way to catch some rainwater.

And if the opportunity ever arose, call for help.

She had other another project too. She'd begun to exercise, trying to make herself stronger by dancing and leaping, but also by push-ups and sit-ups. On her meager diet, exercise made her hungrier. But Lyda persevered. When she was ready to run, she wanted to be able to run far and fast. When she was ready to fight, she wanted to make it count. *I am warrior princess Lyda,* she thought grimly, jumping over the mattress and back again, playing one-legged hopscotch on the stones of the floor, doing stretches and strength exercises and anything else she could thin k remember from her long-ago days as a soccer player, a student, a real person in the real world.

She worked mostly in the evenings, after Victoire had gone and dinner had been eaten. It was high summer now and the days grew languorously long. During the day, Lyda stayed longer and longer in the square of sunlight. One hot, bright day she rolled up the sleeves of her shirt to catch more sun and to stay cool.

She forgot about her sleeves and her bare arms until Jason stopped dead in the doorway.

"What have you done?" he said in a thunderous voice.

Staring wildly around, Lyda said, "I don't know, sir."

"Cover your arms," he roared. "Shameless. Shame!"

Her arms? Her arms! Lyda tugged frantically at the rolled-up sleeves and felt a seam tear beneath her suddenly trembling fingers.

He crossed the room in two steps and struck her across the face in rage. Lyda's cry was trapped in her throat as the hand came back across her mouth. She bit down a second cry as he reached for her, his hand falling again and again as she twisted and turned away to escape. He caught her collar and dragged her up and she went limp, her arms over her head to protect her face.

Her dead weight threw him off balance and he stumbled and let her go and she rolled away from him, feeling the blood from her face and seeing it on his hand as he stood over her, drawing it back to hit her again.

He was grunting as he hit her, in a rhythm that was horribly familiar. Then he saw the blood on his hand too, and stopped abruptly.

His face had the blank, straining look of someone focused elsewhere, and his breath came in
hard gasps.

She hadn't made a sound after the choked
cry. Hadn't begged. Hadn't screamed.

She'd known it would excite him. He would
be on her as if she were a wounded animal. He
would finish the kill. . . .

Or worse.

"You," he rasped. "You made me do that.
You . . . you did it. You whore. You wanton.
How can you ever be trusted?"

"I'm sorry, sir," she forced out. Her mouth
was full of blood. He'd split the inside of her lip
against her teeth. Her cheek throbbed and she
thought she might be in shock.

No one had ever hit her before.

"Am I such a failure that you cannot learn?"
he went on. "Are you so weak that you cannot
learn?"

"No, sir. No sir," she said. She felt blood
dribble from her lips.

"Should I just give up?" He spoke almost as
if to himself.

"No sir," she said, and then, hating herself, selling her soul, "Please, sir."

The silence drew out between them.

She dared a glance up. He was smiling, an odd little smile. "Please sir *Father*," he corrected her.

"Please sir, Father," she said to the floor.

"Stand up," he said.

She stood. She was trembling all over. He reached out and touched her and her shudder of revulsion was hidden in the tremors that shook her. The world spun viciously.

His thumb moved across her chin, once, twice, three times.

He was still breathing heavily, but the quality of the breathing had changed. He was not panting with rage or exertion. He was drawing in deep breaths of pleasure. Of ecstasy.

He cupped her chin. He stroked his thumb through the blood there.

After an eternity, he pulled his hand back. "Good girl," he said. "It's not the end of the world. You'll try harder tomorrow."

"Yes, sir," she said through swollen lips.

"And . . . ," he prompted.

"Thank you, sir."

"Sir," he said. "My child, you must not hold a grudge for what you bring upon yourself."

"Th-th . . ." She stopped. She couldn't breathe. She tried again, "Thank you, Father."

"Child, my child," he said, his voice gentle and kind.

He stayed for a long, long time, stroking her face. When he left at last, she fell to the floor and lay there for a long, long time.

· 18 ·

Five cygnets, she thought, staring numbly from the window. Only five now. She felt a surge of anger. How could the parent swans be so careless with their children?

But it wasn't their fault. She knew that. Some things existed in the world against which one was helpless, not matter how hard one tried.

Her split lip was almost well. The bruises on her face had probably faded to invisibility. But she could feel them still. She thought she would feel them all her life.

Worse, she would feel his thumb on her chin, stroking, stroking, stroking. . . .

Focus, she told herself, and levered the chip of stone against the window. The little pane of glass was very loose now.

She stopped. It could go at any moment, and then what? Involuntarily she glanced over her shoulder, although it was long past time for anyone to visit her. The last couple of weeks had been almost tranquil. She'd filled page after page with self-recrimination, and self-loathing, blaming herself for her beating, talking of her sympathy for anyone who had to deal with such a stupid girl as herself.

She'd almost believed it. If she hadn't been so careless, so stupid . . . It was all her fault. All her fault.

No. That was no good. To believe that would be to believe him. She hadn't asked for it. Not any more than one of the cygnets. Or her sister.

Her sister.

Lyda had been very, very careful not to make any mistakes in the Book of Obedience. When Jason came for her lessons, she spoke only when he spoke to her. She hadn't even responded to Victoire's taunts.

Today, he'd reached out to touch her again, to stroke his thumb across her cheek.

"There, there," he said. "Don't be too hard on yourself. I care for you too much to let you make such terrible mistakes, but I care for you too much not to forgive you too. It's all in the past now. Are we agreed?"

"Thank you, sir," she'd mumbled.

The thumb stopped, then resumed its course across her cheekbone. She knew that she was trembling again. She couldn't help it.

"My child," he said.

"I'm sorry, Father, sir," she said. "Thank you, Father, sir."

"My child," he said again in an indulgent tone, and mercifully, lowered his hand from her face.

She'd washed her face with the cold water and the ragged nub of harsh soap, scrubbed and scrubbed at it. But she didn't think she would ever be clean again.

"Time to go," she said. She had to escape. She had to get away. Next time he touched her, she wouldn't be able to take it. And then she would die—or he would make her wish she had.

She wedged the chip of stone back into the crack in the rock, where it would not show, and watched as the swans made their stately way back to their nest, pausing to feed, the cygnets tipping forward into the water in a comically serious imitation of their parents.

Now she was afraid of the dark. If he came to her in the dark, what would she do?

She turned away from the window and went to the bed and huddled there and waited for sleep or death and almost didn't care which came for her.

He came that night. How had she known he would? She heard the step outside the door and sat up, holding the blanket against her as if it might protect her.

The step was not repeated. But she sensed him, waiting outside the door. She imagined him peering at her through the hidden peephole, using a nightscope, watching her terror and finding pleasure in it.

"Who's there?" she squeaked, and then, more firmly and loudly, "Who's there!"

No one answered her.

If that was Jason, why didn't he come in? If it wasn't Jason, who was it?

He sent someone to kill me, she thought.

"Who are you?" she shouted. "Answer me." If it was Jason, that would cost her pages in the Book of Obedience.

But no one answered.

She waited, taking short, silent, shallow breaths and realized as she did that she was saying on each breath, *Pleasepleasepleaseplease.*

Please.

The steps began again—moving away, down the stairs. She could breathe again.

The next day she was careful to sit a little farther away from Jason. She coughed and sniffled, and he flinched. "I'm sorry, sir," she said. "Maybe I'm catching a cold."

He frowned at her. "How could you?"

"I don't know, sir. I'm sorry, sir." She cleared her throat.

He stood up. Holding the book with only his fingertips, he handed it to her. He wiped his hands on his handkerchief, but she knew later he would be washing them compulsively.

"Feel better," he said, and left her safely alone.

The steps came that night too. She called out again, and again there was no answer. But somehow she was less afraid this time. When the footsteps retreated, she listened carefully. Panic had deafened her the previous night, but now she could tell the footsteps were not familiar. They were not Jason's footsteps, nor Victoire's.

They belonged to someone new, a third visitor. Someone else knew she was here, someone who came at night when they wouldn't be seen, someone who wanted to keep the visits a secret.

She would wait and see. And then she almost laughed.

What else could she do?

Jason did not come the next day. Victoire put the food down and backed away as if Lyda were a leper. Lyda coughed and watched the disgusted face IckVick made. It was funny, but it was sad, too. He'd made her into his image. For the first time, Lyda wondered what would happen to Victoire without her father.

What had happened to Victoire with her father?

She could imagine, imagine enough.

On the third night, Lyda was waiting by the door when her visitor came. She didn't call out this time. She didn't shout or demand. As if she were continuing a normal conversation, she said, "Hello? Hello, my name is Lyda. Lyda Marling. I'm . . ." She paused, thinking. If it was a trap, she could be punished. The beating had taught her that the punishments were getting more severe, more out of control. "I'm locked in here," she said, and added silently, "for eighty-seven days."

The voice that answered at last was familiar. "Lyda?" said Jon. "Lyda, is that you?"

"Jon!" she cried. She was saved. "Jon, help me! Get me out of here."

There was a pause, then Jon said, "Lyda?"

"Yes. It's me. Get me out of here!"

"The door has a lock on it."

"Then break it."

"I don't think I can. . . ."

"Yes, you can! Try! Just try!"

She stopped. Jon. Jon who was Jason's son, Victoire's sister. The son and the brother of madness.

"What are you doing here?" Jon said. She heard his hands on the lock, heard him fumble and curse.

"Jon," she whispered.

"How did you get in there?" he asked.

That stopped Lyda. She tried to think. She said slowly, "Your father brought me here."

"My father?"

"Yes."

"No," he answered flatly.

"Do you think I locked myself in here?"

Now he was silent. Then he said, "No. No, I can see that you didn't."

"Your father brought me here. I thought he was taking me back to school after . . . after the funeral. But it might have made him a little . . . He wasn't himself, Jon, not thinking. He put me in here and . . ."

"You've been here since your sister's memorial?" Jon's voice rose in incredulity. "No!"

"I have. I really have. . . . I'm telling the truth, Jon. You've got to believe me." She paused, tried to think. This was her chance to escape. This was her chance to stop Jason. She was arguing for her life. But trying to find a way to tell Jon—to tell Jason's own son—what had happened made her realize how impossible it must sound.

"Jon," she said, choosing her words slowly, "listen to me. Your father is . . . I think he's . . . had some kind of breakdown. He's . . ."

"He's my father," said Jon.

"Jon," she said. "I'm telling the truth. How else could I have gotten in here? I've been here with only the food and water they bring me. No light, nothing. All alone."

"I know my father," Jon answered.

How could she make him see, make him understand? Or maybe making him understand wasn't what was important, at least not at the moment. "You've got to believe me. Or . . . or even if you don't believe me, you can believe

I'm crazy, if you want. Just let me out of here.
You've got to let me out of here."

Jon said, "I know what my father's capable of."

She wasn't sure she'd heard him right.

"Jon?"

"I . . . Lyda. I'm sorry. I'm so sorry."

He believed her. He believed her! She
wanted to cry. She leaned against the door,
feeling week with hope and relief and a bitter
kind of joy. "Oh, Jon," she said. "Jon, it's not
your fault. "It's not your fault. But you have to
help me. If you can't break the lock, go for
help."

The silence lengthened. For an awful
moment, she thought he'd gone. Then he said,
"You really think I can let you out?"

She froze. It had been a trick. Jon was part of
the plot.

"Jon," she whispered. "Jon, no. You can . . ."

"I can't," he said.

She stopped talking. Jon said, very softly, "I
thought I heard something." He paused again.
Then he said, "Lyda, listen. He follows me. He
has me watched. I can't even trust my friends

at school. Even here, someone is always watching, waiting, reporting back to him. . . . Stinch will do whatever he says, and Stinch is ruthless."

Trick? Or truth? She had to trust him. No matter what it cost, she had to trust Jon. She had to make him trust her. *Keep him talking,* she thought, and asked, "How did you find me, then? Why didn't you say something when you were here before?"

"What are you talking about? I haven't been here before. I just got here this afternoon."

A cold finger seemed to touch her heart. "You just got here?"

"From school. This afternoon. I . . ." He stopped again. He said, "I have to go. Now."

"Jon? Jon, wait!"

"Don't tell anyone I was here," he said. "If you tell him you talked to me, that I know where you are, you'll never get out of here alive. We'll both be dead."

"Jon!" she said, but instinct kept her voice low.

"Dead . . . ," he said, his voice fading. He was leaving!

"Jon," she whispered. "Jon."

But the only answer was the whisper of his footsteps down the winding stairs of the tower.

19

Lyda curled on her bed and thought, *He didn't say he wouldn't be back*. And then she thought, *He didn't say he would*.

She heard a footfall, cautious and stealthy, on the stairs and sat up, thinking for one wild moment it was Jon come back to save her. Then she knew it wasn't, and hope turned to despair and then fear.

Because she knew then that her night visitor had to be Jason.

She lay back down and pulled the blanket over her head so if he watched, he couldn't see her. She was shivering again. Could he

see how she shook, even under the blanket?
Gritting her teeth, she willed herself to still-
ness.

If it is Jason, she thought, *what does he
want?*

She thought of his hand against her face,
and gritted her teeth harder. That touch had
been worse than his fists, far worse. . . .

Desperately she tried to remember the two
nights he'd visited. She'd called out, asked for
help. *Stupid,* she cursed herself. *Stupid.*

Maybe it wasn't too late to fix it. Maybe she
could . . .

She threw back the covers. "Is someone
there? Who's there?" she cried, not having to
pretend to make her voice shaky.

No one answered, of course. "Whoever you
are, go away!" she said.

The silence stretched out.

"Go away!" she said. "Or I'll tell my . . . my
father! He takes care of me, and you'll be sorry,
whoever you are."

She waited. And waited. And at last, the
faint, stealthy steps retreated.

She was safe. For one more night, she was safe.

Safe in a tower where she had been locked in by a lunatic.

He pushed open the door and she rolled away from the sunlight where she had been half-dozing in a stupor. Would he take the sunlight away if she knew how she loved it? She thought he might.

She was tired. So tired. The night before had left her drained and empty.

Jason placed the chair just so and sat down. He regarded her sternly, and she lowered her eyes. He never changed: handsome, immaculate, and horrible.

A vampire sucking out her soul.

She said, "Good morning, sir," as he had taught her.

"Good morning, Lyda." He held out his hand.

Keeping her eyes lowered, she placed the book in it. She'd filled most of the pages. It would be time for another book soon.

"Sir," she said, "I'm sorry. I would have

written more, but I didn't get much sleep last night. I had . . . I had bad dreams. . . ."

"Bad dreams. The just and the pure do not have bad dreams."

"No, sir. I . . . I thought I heard someone outside my door. It scared me. I called for help, and then I realized no one could hear me. I told whoever it was to go away. I was so afraid." She wrapped her arms around herself to emphasize the point, letting her head droop. "So afraid," she whispered. She glanced up, then down again. "This is the third time it had happened. I was so afraid. . . ."

Did he believe her? His hand came out to stroke her hair. "Poor Lyda," he said. "Bad dreams. You must never be afraid. I'll take care of you. Say it."

"You'll take care of me, sir," she said. If she turned her head, just a little, she could bite that hand. Bite the hand that fed her. Bite the hand that touched her. Bite off that thumb. . . . She clamped her lips together.

He made a disapproving noise, and she said quickly, "You'll take care of me, Father. Sir."

"Good girl," he said, and she was reminded of Pan, the lost dog. Pan was bad and he got rid of her, Victoire had said, showing no emotion at all. Had she had other pets and lost them? Lyda understood now that Jason would allow no competition for attention, not even from a dog.

Jason went on, "I've brought you a surprise. Another book. We still have a great deal of work ahead of us, you know." He was being the jovial professor now.

Good girl, she thought. She hoped her ruse would keep him away now at night—at least for a little while longer.

"I sense you are still deficient in things of the heart," he was saying.

"Things of the heart," she repeated, thinking, *what the hell?*

"Yes. The young can be careless that way. But we are going to remedy that. You are going to learn to practice a wonderful art."

He paused, and she said, "Yes sir."

"Letter writing," he announced.

"Yes, sir," she said.

"Not e-mails, but real letters," he said. "To me."

She glanced up, looked back down.

"Yes, to me. To say thank you. To show me how much you appreciate what I am doing for you. To show your devotion. Your love."

Lyda didn't answer. She couldn't. It was ludicrous. Horrifying. Disgusting.

When the silence told her she was expected to answer, she said, "Instead of writing in the Book of Obedience, sir?"

"No. In addition to it. We'll go over each letter as we do each entry in your book, making the appropriate corrections. That's what your new notebook is for. You will write the letter into this notebook, just as you write each entry into your Book of Obedience. Do you understand?"

"Yes, sir," she said.

The lesson that day did not go well. She was slow and stupid and she couldn't help herself. He was shaking his head as he stood to go, and Lyda braced herself. But he went without speaking, leaving the new notebook behind.

That night, no one came, not Victoire, not Jason.

Not Jon.

She was used to hunger by now. She could handle being alone well enough. But she had not been used to hope, and the loss of the momentary hope that Jon had brought was as bad as anything she had ever felt. She groped her way to the window and stared out at the night. She could see stars above the dark shape of the mountains. She could see tiny, almost invisible lights twinkling in the windows of Northwind.

She wondered if one of those lights was in Jon's room. She focused all her thoughts on him. *Come back,* she told him. *Come back.*

But he didn't.

Dear Father,

Thank you for everything you have done for me. I know it hasn't been easy to be patient, but I am grateful that you care for me enough to work so hard.

You sick bastard.

I have been working as hard as I know how to be the person . . .

No.

woman?

No.

*young lady you want me to be, but I am going to find a
way to . . .*

kill you

work even harder to earn your respect and love.

Lyda wrote on: pretend Lyda writing a pretend letter to a pretend human.

To a madman.

He'd said she had shown no gratitude, no
affection for her father who had done so much
for her.

She wondered how he expected her to show
gratitude and affection.

She was afraid she knew. The thought made
her stop and cross her arms across her chest
protectively.

Was that what it would take to escape?

Forcing the thought away, she turned back to the letter. She finished it and licked dry lips. Out in the real world, it had been a long, unusually hot summer. Almost no rain had fallen. The pond had shrunk and the grass was brittle and dry. Even the leaves drooped on the trees.

The night gave the lie to the days, though. Each night was a little cooler, a little longer. High summer was over. She couldn't stay here when it got colder. She wouldn't survive.

She closed the Book of Letters. She closed the Book of Obedience.

She waited.

She passed the next day's lesson well enough, she supposed, because Victoire came with dinner that afternoon. The girl was in an unusually talkative mood. She placed the food near the middle of the room and then stood by the door staring at Lyda.

Lyda tried not to stare at the food.

"You look terrible," Victoire said. "You should take better care of yourself. Daddy doesn't like girls who are careless in their appearance."

If it hadn't been so awful, Lyda might have laughed. "I don't have a mirror, so I don't know how I look," she answered.

"Jon's here visiting before he goes back to school," Victoire said.

"Jon!" Lyda said involuntarily.

"You liked Jon, didn't you? But if he saw you now, he wouldn't think you were so great."

Lyda shrugged.

"He never even asked about you. He didn't like *you* very much."

"So?" Lyda said.

Victoire frowned.

Lyda added, "It's only important that my father approve of me."

"He's not your father!" Victoire flashed. "He's mine. Mine!"

Like her father, Victoire didn't want to share. Lyda fought the urge to say, *You can have him.* But she didn't have to. Because Victoire turned and stormed out, slamming the door behind her.

Did she look so awful? Jason had provided a

toothbrush and foul-tasting toothpaste. Part of the ritual of his visits included Lyda showing him those utensils, she supposed, to prevent her from filing the plastic shaft of the toothbrush into a point for a weapon.

It doesn't matter how I look, she thought tiredly. If she'd changed outwardly, the inward changes matched. The Lyda she had been was gone forever. Jason had seen to that. He hadn't made her over into his ideal image, but he'd succeeded in eradicating who she had been.

She wasn't sure who she was anymore.

But it didn't matter. . . . She'd never see Jon or anyone ever again.

Lyda went to the window to watch the swans, finding comfort in them as always. . . . They'd grown so fast, from downy balls of brown fluff to gawky halflings. One day soon they would be grown and beautiful and would fly away.

Take me, she thought. *Take me with you.* But the swans couldn't save her. It would take a miracle.

Jon came that night.

She didn't believe her ears at first, hearing her name whispered in the dark. She hadn't heard him climb the stairs. She leaped up and approached the door.

"Who's there?" she said cautiously. Was it a trick? A trap?

"Jon," he said. "It's Jon."

"Jon!" she cried, forgetting to whisper.

"Shhh! Listen, I don't know if I can come back. I think he's onto me. I'll try to . . ."

He stopped. Then he muttered, "Damn," and then, "I'm sliding some things under the door for you. It's not much, but maybe it will help. I'm leaving day after tomorrow. Early. I'll try to come back. Don't give up, okay?"

She heard a scraping and scrabbling and ran her fingers along the lower edge of the door. Her fingers touched small boxes, two with plastic on them.

She gathered them up carefully. "Jon?" she said.

But he didn't answer. He was gone.

20

Two books of wooden matches. A package of birthday candles. The nub of another candle. Five packets wrapped in plastic wrap and then foil, which proved to be cocktail nuts.

As the sun rose, Lyda stared at the odd assortment and then thought, *He stole these from the kitchen.* She imagined him creeping down there in the middle of the night, scrounging for things that might not be missed. Or pretending that he wanted a drink of water or a late snack for himself.

Jon, she thought, and was filled with a strange joy. But she checked herself, forced herself to concentrate on what was important now.

Foil and plastic. Hide it, for one thing.

She'd gotten better at hiding things in the nooks and crevices in the stone. She rewrapped the nuts in the foil and hid them. She wrapped all but two of the candles and both books of matches in the remaining plastic, keeping two matches out, then hid those as well.

She slid the two candles and the two matches she had saved into the lining of her coat.

That night with hungry delight she watched the tiny candle burn. The flickering flame delighted her. She felt like a child. She recklessly let the candle burn all the way down, enjoying the extravagance.

She wasn't alone in the dark anymore.

And that night, Jon came again. She heard him and slid from her bed across the floor, the width of which she knew by heart, in daylight or dark. She leaned her head against the old wood and said, "Is it you?"

"It's me. Jon," he said.

He was right there, right on the other side of the door, just inches away. She brought her hand up to rest on the door next to her cheek. "Jon," she breathed. "Thank you for . . ."

"Wait. I think I . . . ," he grunted. Lyda heard scraping and metal on metal. She felt the door vibrate beneath her cheek and hand and raised her head.

"Jon?" she said, and then she realized what he was doing. He was forcing the lock!

A wild excitement ran through, a madness of hope and terror. For a moment, she almost wanted him to stop. For a moment, she was the caged animal that Jason had been trying to create, crouching in her pen, refusing to come out to freedom and safety and life.

Then she was away, grabbing her coat, her shoes, dressing with shaking hands and a pounding heart.

She heard the lock break, heard it fall.

Then the door opened and Jon said, "Hurry! Hurry! You've got to hurry!" The beam of a flashlight blinded her for a moment, and she heard Jon suck in his breath.

"Lyda," he breathed. "Lyda."

"I'm fine," she said. "I'm fine." She ran toward him.

He turned the flashlight and ran down the stairs. She was close behind him. She would be free. Jon would help her find her way, he'd be her witness, together they would stand against the monster that was Jason Ducat, they . . .

He thrust open the door at the bottom of the stairs and she followed him into the clean, clear free night.

Something dark came out of nowhere and Lyda heard the smack of flesh on bone. Jon fell without a sound. The flashlight rolled away.

She wasted precious time staring at it, almost reaching for it. Then she turned to run away, anywhere, turned like a coward to leave Jon to his fate.

Huge hands caught her and swung her up. She gasped and struggled, fighting tooth and nail.

Her captor said, "Mr. Ducat will not be happy with you, Mr. Jon."

Stinch.

"Stinch! Let me go," Lyda said. She tried to make her voice imperious, commanding. It came out a desperate plea.

He didn't answer. He twisted her around until her arms were pinned, and then, as if she weighed nothing, he carried her back into the tower.

She fought. She fought the whole way. She tried to kick against the wall and push them both over and down the stairs. She might fall to freedom. She might fall to her death. She was beyond caring. She screamed now, screamed and kicked and bit, and Stinch carried her upward, upward, into hell's attic. He thrust open the door and dropped her hard.

Lyda tried to scramble to her feet, but Stinch caught her arms and tied them together. Then he tied her legs together and linked her legs to her arms so her back arched in a painful bow.

He left her there.

She screamed again and again, screamed words she didn't know she knew and cursed

Jason and every god she could name. She screamed until her throat was raw and she could shout back the darkness no more.

Later, much later, long after the feeling had left her hands and feet, she heard Stinch come back and fasten another lock on the door.

Victoire freed her the next day, cutting the twine that bound her with a knife that she also used to cut into Lyda's skin, although Lyda didn't feel it or realize it until long after Victoire had left.

Victoire skipped nimbly out of reach, but Lyda could barely move. She groaned in spite of herself as she sat up.

"You were bad," said Victoire. "You tricked Jon into trying to help you escape."

"I didn't trick anybody, you psycho bitch." Lyda was beyond caring. Jason would do to her whatever he planned on doing no matter what she said or how she acted now.

"Oh!" said Victoire.

"You didn't bring food. Or water. So what do I care? Go back and lick your father's boots, you useless little tool." Lyda rubbed her wrists as the pain of feeling begin to burn back into her hands and arms.

"You'll be sorry," said Victoire.

"Sorry? No. Sorry is not the word."

Jon. What would happen to Jon? Or maybe it had been a trap after all. A test, to see if she'd run. Well, she'd failed that test. Big "F" for effort.

She had no food or water for three days.

She wrote in the books. Wrote and wrote and wrote. Wrote incoherently and insanely. Scratched and crossed out and tore at the pages with her pencil.

She lay in the sun and thought about nothing at all. She watched the swans and noticed, in some distant, dead corner of her mind, that an unusual number of cars seemed to be coming and going at Northwind.

On the fourth night, Victoire came. She brought bread and water. She said, "My father was going to come punish you, but he's been too busy."

She waited, but Lyda asked nothing.

"You're not important anymore, you know," Victoire said.

Lyda lay on her bed and thought of Jon falling. Of Lilli falling. Of the tower falling, falling on Jason and Victoire and Stinch, and yes, even herself. It would hurt and then it wouldn't and she would be free.

"He never loved you. He just wanted me to have a sister," Victoire said.

"Who would want to be your sister?" Lyda said. "Unless, of course, she was beaten and locked in a tower."

With a flash of her eyes, Victoire said, "He's found someone else. Someone better. Much better than you." And of course slammed the door as she left.

Bread and water and no company except Victoire, full of secrets and importance and all too easy to drive into a rage and out of the tower.

Did Jason think he was punishing her by his absence? Or was he trying to make her suffer as she waited to see what her punishment would be?

Or was this it? Bread and water forever? Slow starvation?

For it was starvation. It was not enough food to live on, even if she stayed motionless the whole day through.

She began to light the candles at night, burning each one for a little while, watching the flame, imagining that it was not a candle, but a fire, a wonderful roaring fire in front of which sat Lilli and Lyda. They were drinking hot chocolate. With whipped cream. Lots of whipped cream. It was snowing outside. But it was warm inside.

Sometimes, she saved her bread and water and had a late meal, pretending she shared it, miraculously transformed into a feast, in front of that same imaginary fire. She was at a picnic. She settled Swan across from her and made conversation, like a child at a tea party with her stuffed animals and dolls. . . .

Each day grew colder than the last. The cygnets began to test their wings, paddling madly across the water but not quite lifting off. Here and there, a leaf burned red amid the summer green.

One night, half-stupefied with hunger, Lyda

lay watching as the candle guttered down. *I should blow it out,* she thought, but didn't. She reached out instead and lifted Swan and tucked her—for she thought of the toy as a girl—beneath her cheek like a pillow.

"Swan," she murmured, and Lilli seemed so close, so close, she could almost smell her perfume. So real. Was she dying, then? Did that mean Lilli would come for her? Come down a tunnel of light to lead her . . .

Lyda sniffed. She sniffed again. She turned her head and pressed her nose hard against Swan and drew in a long, deep breath. It was real. The scent of her sister's perfume was faint and far away, but it was real.

How was that possible?

"Lilli?" she said aloud, and almost expected an answer.

Of course no one answered. Yet the perfume was there—elusive, but there. She squeezed Swan, and the scent was stronger. Had the starvation heightened her senses? Made her smell things that weren't there, believe things that weren't real?

No.

No. It was Swan who smelled like Lilli.

"Lilli," said Lyda, inhaling deeply, crushing the toy to her face as if she could make Lilli closer still.

She felt it then. In the soft stuffing, she felt a hard object. She heard too, the crinkle of paper.

Holding Swan away from her, she examined the toy.

Was it a squeaker that didn't work? No, it wasn't one of those toys. Turning the stuffed bird over and over, Lyda found a tiny row of slightly different colored stitches under one wing.

With growing excitement, Lyda slid a ragged fingernail along the stitches and at last succeeded in loosening one. She pulled the thread loose and poked her finger inside the toy. She felt it immediately—a folded piece of paper and something more. Carefully, Lyda extracted the tiny square of paper, and then, then, with unsteady fingers, the hard, square object.

Another box of matches? Lyda stared. What was this?

Lyda unfolded the note. It was in her sister's handwriting, dated one week before Jason had come to school and told Lyda that Lilli was dead. A chill pricked Lyda's spine.

She read:

Duck, it's me. I hope you get this. I made a mistake with Jason. A bad mistake. I think he killed both his wives. I think he is going to kill me. He is a jealous, crazy man and I have to leave. When it is safe, I will come for you. <u>Do not trust Jason.</u>

Love, L

And then:

P.S. Here are some matches. Burn this.

Lilli! Lilli was alive. Jason hadn't killed her.

Or had he?

Had Lilli gotten away in time? Had she escaped? Had she known she was going to die and thought to protect Lyda?

No. No, Lilli had known she was in danger

and she had found some way to escape. Lyda was sure of it.

Maybe that was why Jason had kidnapped her. One of the reasons, anyway. Maybe he was trying to lure Lilli out, bring her back to him.

Or maybe he didn't know she had escaped. That she'd fallen and miraculously survived.

Or what if she had faked her own death?

Lyda almost smiled, thinking of that. It was the sort of thing Lilli would like, the dramatic faux exit, knowing she would return to astonish them all.

Yes, thought Lyda fiercely. *Lilli made it. Lilli is free. Free! Alive and free.*

Lyda didn't burn the letter. She hid it along with the matches.

Lilli was alive. Lyda stayed awake from the joy of it all night long. She smiled in her dreams as she slept in the sun that day. She smiled at Victoire and made the girl scowl.

"Give Jason my love," she said as Victoire was leaving. "Tell him I miss him."

The door slammed, and she watched the

dust shake from its boards. She smiled as the golden motes danced in the late afternoon light.

Lilli was alive. That was all that mattered, all she could think about.

That, and escape. She had to escape and find Lilli.

She'd failed once, by bad luck or by cruel design. She wouldn't fail again.

She thought and thought, circling the room, examining everything over and over, a loose stone, a rusted window bar. . . .

No, none of that would work. She stared out at the house, where cars came and went. She squinted and wondered at the sight of a van that looked as if it had flowers painted onto the side.

A florist?

A funeral?

Her funeral?

No. She pushed the thought away. *Focus,* she told herself. *Focus.*

She stared at the fading afternoon fire of the

sun. She thought of the tiny fire of the candle. She saw the glowing logs of that imaginary fire where she and Lilli sat safe and warm.

Wood. Fire.

Lyda turned to stare at the door—the massive, unbreakable, wooden door. The wood was old. And dry. With enough kindling, surely it would burn.

It was a crazy plan, but it might work. With enough candles and matches, she might be able to make a very nice fire. She could try to burn the door down. That could work.

Fire. She would escape by fire.

And then she would find Lilli and send Jason straight to hell.

· 21 ·

Lyda waited through the long night, turning the plan over and over. She would have only one chance. If she failed, she would never escape.

If she failed, she thought now, she would die. Just as she was certain Rebecca had died. Just as Jason's first two wives might have—almost certainly did—at his hands.

She would burn down the door. She would escape. She would run for her life into the woods. She would survive, somehow, find a house, and find the police.

That day, Victoire came like a sleepwalker into the room.

Lyda turned from the window and said, "Who's the party for?" For the cars and trucks had been coming and going all day.

Victoire's eyes widened. "How did you know?" she said. The she caught herself and said, "What party?"

Lyda laughed. "Party or funeral," she said. "From all the trucks and cars visiting Northwind. And people. Guests, right. No one's died here since your father killed Rebecca, right? So it must be party."

"He didn't kill Rebecca!" Victoire burst out. "She left. He fired her."

Lyda shrugged. "No one else dead? Party, then. I love a party! When is it going to be?"

Victoire suddenly smiled. "This weekend. Tomorrow afternoon. In the garden. Too bad you can't come."

A party! It couldn't be better.

Trying to conceal her elation, Lyda said, "Is Jon invited?"

Victoire made a face. She didn't answer.

Lyda felt her heart sink. Jon was in trouble then. Was he a prisoner as she was? She forced herself to speak carelessly, "Stuck at school and had to miss the party. Poor Jon."

"He'll be here," Victoire bit out. But she didn't sound entirely sure.

Jon. Had it been a trick? Or had he paid an awful price when he'd tried to help her escape?

Jason wouldn't kill his own son, would he?

And then a thought struck her with such force, she knew it had to be true. "A wedding party! That's it, isn't it? A new bride to replace the one your father murdered?"

Victoire said, "Shut up."

"Or what? You'll tell Daddy? He won't believe you. He'll know you're just jealous."

"Jealous? Of you? You'll never get out here. Never."

"I'd rather die here than live like you," Lyda said, suddenly tired, her anger suddenly gone. Victoire didn't know any better. She was Jason's daughter, Jason's creation.

Lyda hated Jason. But now she pitied Victoire.

As if sensing her pity, Victoire drew back.

"You want to die here?" she asked. "Good. You'll get your wish!" And she was gone.

Lyda barely noticed.

A party, she thought. A wedding party. How arrogant of Jason.

People. Lots of people.

I think I will try to make it to the wedding, Lyda thought, and smiled.

Tomorrow, she thought. Tomorrow she would live.

Or die.

She spent the day getting ready for the party. All morning long, she picked at the seams of the mattress, tearing at it until at last she split it open. It was a horrible, ancient mattress. She hoped it was so old that it wasn't fire resistant. She dragged the mattress to the door, pulling the stuffing out. She tore her clothes into strips, then melted candle wax and rubbed the wax into the strips of cloth. She laid the wax strips across the mattress, stuffed the mattress full of more clothes, and threaded the stuffing with more wax strips.

She tore paper from the Book of Obedience and the Book of Letters and twisted it into knots so it would burn longer and stuffed that into the mattress too. Finally, she rubbed all the remaining wax along the door, streaking the old wood with the last of the birthday candles.

When she was satisfied, she rested in the sun, getting up from time to time to check on the progress of the party.

She watched the cygnets practice and thought, *I'll miss them.* But the moment had come for all of them to fly away.

At last it was time. She washed her face and hands and tied her ragged hair back with a strip of cloth, making a careful knot so that none of it floated free around her face. She laid out her pants and shirt and coat and two pairs of socks and her only pair of shoes in the middle of the room. She tucked Swan into one coat pocket and put what was left of the water nearby.

Then she crouched by the mattress and, with shaking hands, struck the first match. It fell from her trembling fingers, hissing out before it landed.

She stared for a moment at the blackened match head, then gave herself a mental shake. *Pay attention,* she told herself. *Focus.*

She lit a second match and lowered it onto a strip of candle-waxed cloth, keeping one hand cupped to protect it from any hint of a draft.

The cloth blackened and curled—and then it caught, a tiny flame licking along it.

Lyda lit a second match, then a third, each time more and more sure of herself. The mattress caught! Reluctantly, but it burned. It burned more beautifully than any fire she had ever seen.

With a mighty shove, Lyda heaved the burning mattress against the door and watched the flames lick up the wood. For one long, awful moment she thought the door would not burn.

But it did, slowly at first and then with a joyous life, the heat of the flames driving her back, back.

Lyda coughed and gasped as the black smoke filled the room and thought, *No, damn it, no, no!*

Eyes streaming, gasping, she groped for one of the pairs of socks, fumbled them over her hands, and ran to the window, turning at the last moment for the one away from the view of Northwind. She hammered at the glass desperately and finally felt it give way and shatter. She broke every pane she could reach, trusting the socks to keep her hands from being cut to ribbons, but not much caring, either.

No time, no time, her brain screamed over and over. She ran back through the haze of smoke and fire to her clothes. Then she took the last of her water and poured it over them and pulled them on, rubbing the damp clothes against her hair and tying a wet strip of cloth over her face.

The door was in full blaze now, and the room was almost black with smoke. She dropped to her knees and crawled toward the fire.

The heat threw her back. She knelt at the edge of it, watching it burn. The world was made of fire and smoke, and her life depended on the fire. The fire could kill her.

She ran at the burning mattress and seized it

and dragged it halfway across the floor before the heat sent her reeling away. Now the door burned alone, and the mattress made its own mirror bonfire in the center of the room.

Lyda knew she couldn't last much longer. She crouched and waited, waited, thinking, *Time, time, time* and then, *Please, please, please.*

Then she leaped up and ran forward and kicked at the lower part of the door as hard as she could. She felt something splinter and give and she leaped back, expecting to be in flames herself. But her wet clothes steamed and smoked yet did not burn.

Panting and gasping, she tore strips of wet cloth from her shirt and tied first one leg and then the other of her pants tightly against her legs, giving herself clumsy wet-bandaged legs against the heat of the fire.

She steeled herself and lunged forward again, kicking and kicking and finally feeling wood shatter. Then she fell back again to bend over, hands on knees, eyes streaming from the smoke, lungs burning, the world burning.

She knew she was in pain, but she couldn't

feel it. The lower half of the door had collapsed into a heap of burning rubble.

A third time, she went forward, kicking and pushing the rubble away before she fell back. This time she did not wait before throwing herself forward a fourth time on her hands and knees to plunge into the ring of fire at the bottom of the door.

She closed her eyes. She felt the flames roar, the fire singe, tried not to breathe. Her coat caught on something, and for one horrifying moment she was trapped in the inferno she had made.

And then she was through, rolling and bouncing halfway down the stairs before she caught herself somehow.

She lay, trying to breathe, trying not to feel. It hurt to breathe. It hurt a lot.

Time, the voice said in her head, and she somehow got to her feet, her hands on the rail, both hands still in the steaming, ragged, scorched socks, and she held on for dear life as she staggered and slipped and fell to the bottom of the tower.

For a moment, she thought she wouldn't have the strength to push the door open, but she did.

She stepped out into the sunlight, onto the grass, and even though it drove a knife into her ribs, breathed.

She ran down the rough track until she came to the road. Then she ran to the road, the driveway to Northwind. She stopped, listening, and thought she heard a car and she plunged into the shadows of the trees.

It was a car. She dropped to her belly as it rounded the curve.

The car was not looking for her, not yet. She recognized the big, ugly SUV and the big, ugly driver. Stinch.

But he wasn't looking for her. Not yet.

Time.

She struggled up and ran on.

She came at last to the sweep of drive that led to the house. She stopped. The pain was far away now, but it was coming. It was coming for her and it would take her if she would let it. But she couldn't, not yet.

Time.

Lyda ran along the edge of the driveway toward the back of the house, followed the way that led to the service entrance, and ducked into the shrubbery.

The garden was just ahead. Just . . . there.

She heard music stop and a voice began to intone words that were familiar and she tried to take a deep breath and almost fell. All the colors were so bright, so blindingly bright, the guests in their hats and wedding finery, the flowers heaped everywhere.

Water, she thought. There would be water.

The voice droned on, pausing. The wedding vows. He stood up there with someone who maybe believed he loved her. He stood up there, murder, torturer, sadist. Bigamist.

Lyda lurched out of the shrubbery and moved forward. She reached the edge of the garden and staggered and almost fell. She grabbed a huge urn of flowers for balance and hung there.

The minister said, "Speak now or forever hold your peace."

Lyda opened her mouth.

She saw heads turn toward her as people become aware of her presence, sensed rather than saw the shock and horror on their faces.

Then a familiar voice rang out nearby, making a grand entrance as only the owner of that voice could.

"I object," said Lilli Marling Ducat. "Jason is already married. To me."

No one spoke. No one moved.

Then, Jason, incredibly, turned and walked down the aisle toward Lilli. "Lilli! Darling!" he cried. "You're alive!"

Lilli didn't move. She stood there, beautiful and perfectly dressed. She was thinner, thinner than Lyda had ever seen her, holding center stage as she watched her murderer come down the aisle.

She waited until he reached her, until he almost had his arms around her, then brought her knee up not once, but twice, hard and viciously and right on target between his legs.

Lilli wasn't big, but she was strong and she had the element of surprise on her side. Not only that, but Lilli's fascination with the martial arts had lasted, Lyda remembered, far longer than her fascination with the black belt stunt double she's once dated. Jason screamed as he fell, clutching himself, and she raised her foot and stomped the four-inch stiletto heel of her designer shoes into him with devastating accuracy and killing rage, intoning a word on each blow: "Where . . . is . . . my . . . sister?"

He screamed, and the crowed was surging around them. Lyda saw Victoire run forward, shouting, "Daddy, Daddy, no, Daddy!"

But she didn't reach him. Jon caught his sister and held her.

"Where . . . is . . . Lyda?" Had Lilli just broken his knee? He writhed and tried to get up, only to fall. The material of his beautiful suit ripped away, but no one came to his aid. The minister seemed to have his hands full with the jilted bride. The guests were too stunned or frightened or interested to move.

She did not raise her voice, but it carried.

Lyda found her own voice at last. She straightened and stepped forward and said, "I'm here. Lilli, I'm here."

Lyda refused to go down to the house. She refused to go the hospital. She refused to even go into the house. She saw by the faces pressing in around her that she looked bad. But she felt good. She felt fine.

She sat obstinately on the chair where Lilli had placed her, watching Lilli, ignoring everyone else.

Jon sat beside her. He held one of her burned hands in his, very, very carefully.

Lilli had not come alone. Detectives and policemen were thinning the wedding herd. Some of the guests had melted away to the reception area and were eating and drinking and watching and talking.

Let them, Lyda thought.

Lilli came to kneel beside Lyda and looked up into her face. Lyda gazed at her sister. "Lilli," she said. "You're so thin. Are you all right?"

Lilli's face puckered for a moment, and her lips trembled. But she smiled and said, "Nothing a little food and spa won't fix, Duck."

"Yes," said Lyda.

Jason was struggling still, staggering, injured, bloody. They'd cuffed him and were leading him away. Lyda stood as he passed by.

He turned his head and saw her.

She stared at him for a long moment. He was a monster. She was human. He would never change. She was changed forever.

But she was still, after all, Lyda. She said, "You broke all the rules, Jason. You'll have to be punished."

The monster's face twisted then, was seen true and clear by all who stood around him. He lunged toward her, and the police dragged him back, still struggling. Foam flecked his lips and his eyes were red as blood and Lyda knew that Jason Ducat was gone forever from this world. The monster would have a cell of his own, smaller than hers.

"Lyda," Lilli said softly. She reached up and pushed back a strand of Lyda's hair.

"I'm going to need a haircut," Lyda said. 'I think I burned half of it off."

"Short is a good look for you," said Lilli. "Haven't I always said it?"

"You're not always right, you know," Lyda said automatically.

She was puzzled by the tears that suddenly welled up in her sister's eyes.

Jon said, quietly, "She needs to go to a hospital."

"Yes," Lilli said, tipping the tears away with her fingertips. She stood and looked around and waved imperiously. "My car," she said. "Bring it right here. No, right here. I don't care if you have to drive over a hundred flower beds."

"I hate hospitals," said Lyda fretfully.

"Who doesn't?" said Jon.

"I'm thirsty," Lyda said suddenly, remembering, and Jon picked up a glass and held it to her lips and she drank and drank.

She didn't remember much about the trip to the hospital. It wasn't a big hospital. She had her own room with a view of a tiny bed-and-breakfast across the road. Jon stayed there, she found out later, when he wasn't taking turns with Lilli keeping watch on Lyda.

They kept her for three days, and she remembered almost none of the first day and a half except that she hurt and then they gave her shots and then she didn't hurt so much. She talked, sometimes, to Lilli or Jon, but she didn't remember what she said. They learned enough, though—things she would never repeat again, things that she would never in her right mind say aloud to anyone.

On the afternoon of the second day, a jolly-looking doctor with a halo of gray curls and jewel-rimmed glasses told her that she could go the next morning.

"You're in good shape, all things considered," the doctor said.

"Yes," said Lyda.

"Undernourished, with burns and contusions, but nothing too serious. Continue with the antibiotics and the bland diet and make sure you are monitored by your own doctor."

"She will be," Lilli said.

"Thank you," murmured Lyda, who planned on never seeing a doctor again.

"Therapy might be useful too," the doctor added, as if an afterthought.

"Yes," said Lilli.

"No," said Lyda.

"You're a brave young woman," said the doctor.

"No," said Lyda.

"Yes," said Lilli.

Lyda said, "I'm hungry."

They ate together, a hospital picnic. The food was awful, but there was plenty of it. The company was very good.

"He tried to kill me," Lilli said. "I knew something was wrong, very wrong. I didn't want to believe it, but after your visit, Lyda, I was certain."

"He killed Rebecca," said Lyda.

"Yes," said Lilli. "I was just told they found her body in the graveyard. She'd been . . . strangled."

Jason's hands against her throat . . . Lyda must have made a sound, because Jon said, "Lyda?"

"I . . . It's awful," said Lyda.

"I didn't know," Lilli said. "When something like that happens, you don't believe it. I knew Rebecca shouldn't have disappeared the way she did, but when I said something to Jason, he said he'd dismissed her. That she'd misread her relationship with him and had become irrationally jealous. 'Unbalanced,' he called her." Lilli's mouth twisted a little at that. "I tried to go on, to act as if nothing was wrong, but Jason became increasingly possessive. He watched me constantly. He wouldn't let me leave Northwind unescorted. If he wasn't with me, Stinch was."

Lilli made a face at the memory. "That's when I started writing you those e-mails, Lyda. I was trying to warn you."

"It was weird, getting them," Lyda said. "It wasn't like you. It didn't sound like you."

"I didn't want to sound like me. I wanted you to be suspicious. I suspected you didn't like Jason and I didn't want you to change your mind. But I couldn't really warn you. He had me cornered."

"Yes," said Lyda softly. She looked over at Jon. "This must be awful for you."

Jon didn't answer. His face was solemn, but calm.

"Jon mailed the swan to you for me. He smuggled it out and mailed it from his school."

"Not the swan. Swan," corrected Lyda, glancing over at the stuffed toy, a bit bedraggled now, that sat on the table next to the bed.

"I finally told Jason I wanted a divorce," Lilli said. "He laughed. He said I was upset. That I needed a vacation. I let him persuade me. We went to Europe. I had two near accidents that could have been fatal.

"That's when I realized he planned to kill me. Two days later, we went hiking in a remote section of the Pyrenees. I went ahead. I pretended to be giddy, happy, careless. I stumbled and slipped and pretended to be afraid. When I got far enough ahead of him, I fell over the cliff into the river below. Far, far below."

"But you didn't fall," said Jon.

"No. I screamed. My pack went halfway down the ravine. My shoe hit a ledge below.

There were skid marks and broken branches and enough evidence to convince most people I was dead. The river is famously dangerous, a bottomless river, they call it. People who go in are often not found for years, if ever.

"I think he planned to push me in. But I'm not sure he believed I fell, at least not at first.

"I went into hiding. And I began to try to figure out what to do about Lyda. And about Jason. I knew no one would believe me. Not unless I had proof. But how could I get proof against someone as rich and powerful as he was? And proof of what? Rebecca's death?

"And then I thought, not just Rebecca's death, but his first two wives, too. . . . I didn't know about you, Lyda, then. I didn't know what he'd done, what he was doing to you."

Lilli stopped, staring down at her hands. Then she said, "I tried to get in touch with you at your school. They told me you'd been withdrawn. They didn't know the name of the school your guardian had transferred you to. They were still waiting to be notified about where to send your record."

"I panicked then. I didn't know what to do. That's when I called Jon."

"He was never my guardian," Lyda said, just to be sure.

"No! Hell, no!" Lilli said.

"He was never my father," said Jon.

Lyda turned. "But . . ."

Jon said, "She was pregnant with me when she married him. He killed her shortly after I was born. I was his only son, but he always acted as if he couldn't stand the sight of me. And I . . . instinctively, I think . . . didn't like him. I never wanted him to love me, never wanted to be like him, never thought of myself as his son. A friend at school whose father is a doctor was able to tell from my blood type. With my blood type, I could never have been his son."

"Oh, Jon," said Lyda.

"I was glad," Jon said fiercely. "Relieved. Because by then, I knew he wasn't right, that there was something very wrong with him. I saw some of what he was doing to Victoire. But I was away at school. He couldn't just dispose of me because I was his son. But he could keep me out of his sight." Jon sighed. "I was lucky. A lot luckier than poor Victoire."

Poor Victoire. The name hung in the air. Then Jon said, "It's a very well-respected institution. She'll get help. She'll never have to worry about money. Or about Jason, ever again."

Lyda didn't say anything. She wondered if Victoire would ever think about anything else. She'd had to be heavily sedated after the wedding. Jason had created her. And he had destroyed her. Lyda wondered if there was anything left inside of Victoire that would allow her to come back to life. *Daddy's little girl.*

She pushed the food away. She'd had enough.

Jon went on, "Lilli couldn't find you. She asked me to help. And when I came home for break, I started watching my father much more closely. I thought maybe I could get into his study when he wasn't around and find out what school he'd put you in, Lyda. But I couldn't find out anything.

"Then I saw Victoire one afternoon. She was so clearly sneaking out of the house that I followed her. She went to the old tower, went in with one bag and came out with another. It was odd, odd enough so I followed her again—twice more. Then that night I went back. When I heard your voice, I couldn't believe it."

"I was so glad to hear yours," said Lyda fervently.

"I wasn't much help."

"You were. You gave me matches and candles. And hope."

"I should have let Lilli know right away. But I thought Jason had caught on to me. And then Stinch caught us trying to escape."

Jon lapsed into silence.

Lilli took up the story again. "Jon disappeared. Just like that. He didn't come back to school. I couldn't reach him."

"He locked you up too," Lyda said.

"Not the way he did you, no," said Jon. "I had a bodyguard, twenty-four/seven. I couldn't leave Northwind. Jason told me if I tried to escape, you would never leave that tower alive. He had me. There was nothing I could do. I'd seen you. I'd seen what he'd already done to you. I didn't know what to do."

Lilli took up the story again. "When Jon didn't come back to school, I knew something was very wrong. So I brought myself back to life. I went to a private detective, a very good private detective, and began to find out everything I could about Jason. And then I read about the wedding and I knew I had my chance to confront him safely."

"We were the unwelcome guests," Lyda said with a snort of laughter.

"No kidding," said Jon. "I've never been so glad to see anyone in my life as I was to see Lilli. Until I saw you, Lyda."

Lyda felt herself blushing. "Oh," she said.

Jon said, "You're amazing, you know that? That stunt you pulled, burning down the door and half the tower? You could have died."

"I didn't," Lyda said. "So it's okay."

"Don't do that again. Promise me. Okay?" Jon said, and then it was his turn to redden and look away.

"Lyda was always the brains in the family," Lilli said complacently. "Smart and beautiful."

"Yes," said Jon, regaining possession of himself.

"Ha," said Lyda.

She was tired now, a good tired. She yawned and lay back on the pillow.

Lilli stood. "We'll leave first thing tomorrow," she said. She stood.

"School starts in two weeks. You need to get in shape to shop."

"Shop," Lyda said almost dreamily. Maryjane was going to go ballistic when she heard what had happened to Lyda.

School, she thought, and then she thought of the tower. She would have nightmares for a long time. But she didn't think anyone would ever be able to frighten her again.

Forensic psychology, she thought, drifting off to sleep. What had Maryjane called it. The study of human monsters. She could almost hear Maryjane's voice. *They exist for a reason,* Maryjane was saying. *Wouldn't you like to know why. . . .*

Lyda fell into a deep and dreamless sleep, in spite of a pillow and a bed that was, given what she'd was used to, much too soft.

● ● ●

It was a bright and sunny day. The car purred along the narrow winding roads toward the airport. Lyda was on her way back into life and she would never take it for granted again. She lowered the window and leaned out, feeling the burn of cold air against her burned face. *Wonderful,* she thought. *Lovely. Perfect. Grand.*

She didn't have enough words in the world for every wonderful thing. Jon would be at his school nearby. And Lilli. Lilli would always be Lilli, unconquerable, unshakeable, loyal and true and beautiful and her sister. Her family.

She felt the sun on her face and closed her eyes and didn't have to imagine she was anywhere else but here.

Then she opened her eyes and stared up. There, outlined against the blue sky, were seven swans: two adults and five half-grown cygnets. They beat against the wind, beginning their journey. The world was theirs.

And hers.

"Good-bye," she whispered, watching them out of sight. "Good luck."

ABOUT THE AUTHOR

D.E. Athkins was born and raised in the haunted South, moved several times only to discover that the living are infinitely more frightening than the dead, and now lives a satisfyingly haunted life in the company of good dogs and good friends, living and dead.